the Last Block
in HarLem

THE LAST BLOCK IN HARLEM

A NOVEL

CHRISTOPHER HERZ

PUBLISHED BY

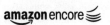

PRODUCED BY

 MELCHER MEDIA

FOR SARUUL—MY LIGHT.

Text copyright © 2010, Christopher Herz
All rights reserved.
Printed in the United States of America

10 11 12 13 14 15 16 / 10 9 8 7 6 5 4 3 2 1

Published by AmazonEncore
P.O. Box 400818
Las Vegas, NV 89140

Produced by Melcher Media, Inc.
124 West 13th Street
New York, NY 10011
www.melcher.com

Library of Congress Control Number
2010905851

ISBN-13: 978-1-935597-04-9
ISBN-10: 1-935597-04-3

This novel was originally published, in a slightly different form, by Canal Publishing in 2009.

Cover design by Ben Gibson
Interior design by Jessi Rymill
Cover source photograph by Greg Flores
Author photo by Saruul Herz, 2010

SUSTAINABLE
FORESTRY
INITIATIVE

Melcher Media strives to use environmentally responsible suppliers and materials
whenever possible in the production of its books. For this book, that includes
the use of SFI-certified interior paper stock.

Dear Reader:

The Last Block in Harlem is a study in contrasts: It's the story of a specific place, but also the story of any neighborhood trying to balance the inevitability of change against the comfort of tradition; the story of a specific set of characters, but also the story of all New Yorkers; the story of trying to do the right thing and the high cost that can sometimes exact.

It all starts with a man (never named) who wants to clean up his street. No grand plan, no hidden agenda—just a guy trying to clean up his street with a broom and a dustpan. Simple enough, right? In the hands of terrific new writer Christopher Herz, what this story snowballs into will sometimes surprise you, sometimes anger you, but always fascinate you.

One of the great joys of the book are the vignettes peppered throughout that illuminate the lives of these New Yorkers. If you're a fan of the snooping, swooping, telescoping fly-on-the-wall style of Robert Altman, you're in for a treat. We meet a wonderfully eclectic cast of characters—some for only a page or two—but all of them indelibly painted and all contributing to a vibrant cacophony of the voices, fears, battle scars, and little victories that make up the people of a city.

And yet, despite that vibrant cacophony, there is a lovely melancholy that wafts its way through *The Last Block in Harlem*. Christopher Herz is a writer who understands not only the pulse of a city but the heartbeat of its inhabitants. I hope you'll enjoy discovering this great new talent as much as I have.

Thanks,

Terry Goodman

Terry Goodman
Senior Editor
AmazonEncore

CHAPTER 1

ST. NICHOLAS PLACE

1

Before I start talking about what I've done, what I've built, and what kind of legacy I've attempted to leave behind, let me first talk about the sounds I thought were haunting me.

The first noise came from the Bodega across the street. I know buildings can't make their own sounds. I'm talking about the people who lived their lives up against that yellow painted wall of the Bodega that stretches between 153rd and 155th Street, with St. Nicholas Place acting as the spine. Whether it was the blasting, static-laced radio that rested on the ice machine or the thumping bass that came from the gold Lincoln Town Car perpetually double-parked in front, the Bodega noises cut through the silence I searched for in the darkness. The second came from above, from the footsteps that pelted the floor of the apartment one story up.

Namuna could sleep through anything, including the sounds that haunted me. When the crowd gathered in front of the Bodega I would open up the window and yell down, but the *thump*, *thump*, *thump* over my head kept me from dreaming.

"It's you who keep yourself from dreaming," Namuna would say when she felt my eyes open next to her. "Don't listen to what you don't want to hear. Have a little discipline, for God's sake." She'd go back to sleep right after dropping her wisdom on me, but I was jumpy and could only concentrate on the echoes that followed me up and down the dark, narrow halls of our fourth-floor walk-up in Sugar Hill, Harlem, USA.

2

I specifically remember November 25, 2006, because of the Sean Bell murders. The date was printed across the top of a newspaper suspended just below the deep tired eyes of the woman next to me at the Laundromat down on 147th. The dryers tumbled loudly behind her. Everyone was standing in front of machines, waiting for others' cycles to stop so they could do their own laundry.

"Fifty bullets. Even if 'e was a very bad man, 'dere is no need for fifty bullets," she said in a heavy Jamaican accent while struggling to hold the newspaper in place.

"I wonder how steel and metal can run with such precision, but humans can't," I said, trying to impress her by capturing a moment in one sentence. When she didn't react, I tried one more. "I mean, we designed these washing machines, no?"

"We designed the violence as well now, didn't we?" she said, capturing the moment—the times, really—with far more skill than I. "These here be the latest murders brought to us by de NYPD. And what a show it 'as been! You'd think dat dis might push da racial tensions high 'round 'ere now, wouldn't you? No, I guess you 'oodn't. Now I suspect dat dere might be some marches, a few speeches, but nobody 'ill be motivated to act. Look 'ere the quote from that councilman of ours."

I felt some of the ink rub off the page onto my fingers as she handed me her copy of the paper.

"This situation requires us to appreciate the volatile nature that arises from the repercussions of passionate reaction," said Councilman Marcus Macon of Harlem. *"I urge the people that hold animosity in their hearts to rally under the leadership of the March Against Police Brutality next Thursday afternoon."*

Posters of Councilman Macon were everywhere to remind folks whom to vote for when the time came around. He had cleaned up the parks and ran off the junkies, but that was before we moved here. Everyone in the neighborhood saw him as a savior and the man who would one day be their mayor.

"Are you going to the rally?" I asked.

"Nothin' dat a rally gonna do ta bring dat man back, is dere?"

"I suppose not," I shrugged. "Though it's a chance to teach the kids a thing or two about how to treat each other."

She took the paper back and folded it up. A small coupon insert fell to the floor.

"I 'ave four sons. Three of 'em be jewels, yes? Computer engineer. Teacher. Lawyer even, they 're. One of them, well, 'e just started drinking dat juice so bad. I tried to get him a job with me up at the Presbyterian Hospital, but 'e couldn't hold it. Now 'e just a drunk. I taught 'im well. It's just the people and influences that're around sometimes can't be resisted. You 'ave children to be speakin' 'bout 'ow to raise 'em?"

A little kid braided the hair of her doll on the chair across from me.

"No, no kids. Not yet."

"Why is dat?" she asked looking me up and down, adding up each of my thirty-five years. "Don't you be wanting to 'ave children?"

"We're not in the right place in our lives yet," I told her.

"How does your wife be feelin' about dat?"

"She wouldn't want anything interrupting her career."

"See now, that there is a big difference 'tween how a man and a woman think. Men be thinkin' it's an interruption, while the women see the blessin'. Not sure 'ow much of a blessin' Ms. Bell be feelin' about 'er boy now though. 'Uch a shame, fifty bullets."

The child had begun braiding her head to look like the doll's. There was a flash of a room in my memory—a room that was supposed to have been serene.

The woman snapping open her paper to read again brought me back to the moment.

"No, I don't have any kids, yet," I replied to a question I had already answered. "Someday though, not too far away. I'd like to try."

"Well, when you do, be sure to come 'round and tell me how you kept 'em out of harm's way. See now, harm 'as its way of jumpin' right in front of you disguised as joy."

The timer on the dryer went off, and I removed my clothes without saying a word, caught between an important conversation and an inescapable memory.

A man sporting a heavy beard and an even heavier bag of laundry walked in and dropped his bundle on the countertop before wiping his forehead clean of sweat. After his last movement, he froze, fixated on my shoes.

"Trade me shoes," he said.

"You want my shoes?"

"Yep, yep—your problems, dude. Your problems for mine?"

"We'd just be exchanging problems then," I said. "Wouldn't do either of us any good."

"I get it. You're a real quick guy with the jokes, dude."

He walked closer, still laughing, but his proximity gave me a whiff of the gin and blunt on his breath. I leaned back slightly and tried to keep him from touching my clothes, but couldn't.

"Come here for a second," he said, his voice just above the whisper he had intended. "I'm going to tell you what I'm thinking."

"I'm in the middle of folding," I told him. "I shouldn't break my concentration. I'm not a very neat person by nature, so it takes some effort to do this."

He glanced toward the woman I had been speaking with earlier, then moved even closer to me. "You want to know what my wife went and said to me? Do you? She said that she was gonna sell her panties because I didn't have enough money for her."

As he backed away and folded his arms squarely, I could actually hear his heart sink over the jangling of quarters around us. The alcohol that was drowning him held his eyes out of focus while he waited for a response.

"Hey. Hey! You not talking to me now?" he yelled. "What should I do? What would you do with that?"

"I . . . I'm not sure she meant it," I said, rolling up my wife's little purple panties and thinking for a moment how faded I would be if she had said something like that to me.

"You ain't got nothing funny to say about that one? You came with some classics before," he said. "Have you heard about me? I'm a soldier. Dude like me won't stand for punks like you." He was looking back toward the door to see if his wife was on the way in. The clothes he was putting in the dryer were still unwashed.

"Where you from, dude?" he asked. "You're an Irish, aren't you?"

"No . . . no, I'm—"

"You're a goddamn Irish if I ever saw one. I've seen plenty."

I hadn't finished folding, but I packed up everything and headed for the door. The man grabbed my hand and shook it against my will.

"We'll meet up soon," he said, his face inches away from mine. "Next time you might have some decency and come correct by asking me my name."

I pulled away and moved quickly toward the door.

"You can holler back at me when you have something to say to me. You want to help me? Want some shoes?"

As the sounds of his yelling mixed with laughter fading away behind me, I was back on my block again, moving toward the small park that divided St. Nicholas Avenue and St. Nicholas Place.

3

Pushing our laundry up the block in one of those metal carts that seems standard-issue for every New Yorker, I felt as free as I would let myself. True, it was a weekend day, but I remember that back then, I was attached to my desk at work even when I wasn't sitting at it. Spending so much time in the office had caused it to become part of me.

From an outside perspective, I knew anyone looking would think that I had *made* it. There were hundreds of other writers who would have lined up to take my position, but they had no idea what it entailed. Working in advertising was putting me on the fast track to madness.

Thing is that to anyone else, my situation represented stability.

SYMPTOMatic®, the company I worked for, had grown and expanded until they were the top ghost agency in New York. Ghost agencies are the ones hired out by the bigger, more established groups—the ones with all the high-profile clients but not enough qualified workers to meet their demands. Clients need a name they can trust, so those big companies land the deals and then farm the work out to smaller agencies like mine, who keep their mouths shut and their pockets filled.

I had been working at SYMPTOMatic® for a year. They had poached me from another agency. Being approached by a group of people to come and work for them, to come and write for them, really got to my ego.

I never wanted to live the life of a writer who struggled to make money. I could always string words together convincingly, and applying the skill to advertising made the most sense to me. I spent too much time as a child watching my mother decide the best way to stretch a dollar, and decided early on that I wouldn't follow that road.

The heart of advertising, the very essence that gives it life, is deception. I think that's why I was so good at it. Growing up in a single parent household—one that hardly resembled the ones in shows or commercials—I was always losing myself in the lives of others. I thought that if I could somehow afford the stuff being sold between shows, I would by extension achieve the smiles and happiness encapsulated in those subjective selling points. I didn't mind being tricked, because it gave me a comfortable reality.

As I saw it, deception, whether perpetrated by religion, politics, or philosophical movements, had distorted the world's reality. I figured that joining the advertising world would give me a chance to play the game for money.

Around the time those sounds started keeping me up at night, here's how I was making a living:

Let's say you're a company that makes cigarettes. Since you're not allowed to advertise your product on mediums like the Internet, what's a huge corporation with unlimited cash flow to do? Well, you turn to an advertising agency to create something called an "unbranded website." This site could be devoted to something like, say, auto racing, with interactive racing games, videos, and biographies of famous race car drivers. There is no mention whatsoever of cigarettes.

So the site gets designed with a blown-out budget because, of course, it's being funded by big tobacco. So who builds the site? Well, the *idea* for the site comes from the huge agency—the one that has been around for more than forty years and gets paid for knowing how to get people to change the way they think. However, while the big agencies love the millions and millions they get, they don't want to be known to the public as the ones responsible for creating a website promoting cigarettes. So what do they do? They farm out the work to smaller agencies that do the work the big agencies are being paid for. Ghost agencies.

How does this site promote smoking? Well, in order to access this site, you need a *password*. How do you get a password? There are codes printed on the bottom of new packs of cigarettes. A few weeks after the site is created, targeted smokers start to receive letters and emails notifying them of a secret website only they can access. All they need to do is enter the code on the pack.

Part of the advertising agency's campaign is to get the word out about the codes through blogs developed for just this purpose. I'd say they hire about twenty kids off Craigslist in every major city to write posts for a week to spread this message alone.

What color are the race cars and the uniforms and the words and layout of the site? Same as the cigarette packs, of course. Do people outside the cigarette-smoking community know about this? No, but who cares? The target audience is enjoying the content provided by the companies and showing their friends. They say, "Cool site, where did it come from?" Word gets out that the codes came from cigarette packs, and boom.

What did I do for these companies? I wrote their business plans, website copy, brochures, marketing decks, web video scripts, taglines—whatever needed words in a sentence, I did it. At SYMPTOMatic®, I was making well above six figures, which allowed Namuna, an assistant architect at a large firm, the time to work her way up the ladder.

It was hard to sleep. I had so much in my head that I couldn't turn off. I felt it pounding from the inside and pushing its way out. I needed to use everything I'd stockpiled in my brain—I couldn't just toss it. With so much lodged in my mind, it was nearly impossible to notice the subtleties of life that presented themselves on a daily basis. That's why it was strange that I detected anything out of the ordinary taking place at the town house I'd passed by twice a day for the nearly two years we had lived on the block.

The FOR SALE sign was nothing new. So many of the places around the block were going on the market. What was out of place was the small groups of sunglass-clad folks holding plastic wineglasses gathered on the stoops taking pictures of whatever they could on their cell phones. Though I worked with these types and laughed with them during business hours because I had to, I always enjoyed the fact that I escaped from them in Harlem.

Growing up on the West Coast, I'd had dreams of bricks and fire escapes. That was success for me. I had no need for the high-gloss lifestyle. My main desire was the purchase of authenticity.

Above the groups a sign read WHAT AN INTERNATIONAL ARTIST CAN DO. I saw a woman with straightened hair and a tight suit simultaneously talking on her BlackBerry, smiling at whom she thought were the right people, and giving orders to the day laborers. She saw me looking at her and took the opportunity to pitch me.

"I'd just love for you to come in and discover what we've managed to do with the space," she said. "Or, I should say, what the *artists we commissioned from around the world* have done. Though I must say it *was* my vision to have them create scenes on each level of this town house in their own distinctive style. The multiculturalism in their design reflects the new dynamic of Harlem. Here's my card."

Her BlackBerry went off again, and she rushed to the door, catching the heel of her Betsey Johnson in the cement and leaving the slightest of impressions.

I looked down at her card, expecting to find the title of art dealer. It read:

BRENDA HAMILTON
REAL ESTATE LIAISON
BROWNSTONE RESTORATION PROPERTIES

"So let me make sure if I understand the situation," said a voice that always broke through whatever clouds were in my head. "I leave you alone for a minute, and women just start handing over their numbers? It's nice to know I own this man."

Namuna had gotten off early and was standing on the step below me on the threshold to the town house, looking up with a smile that was only for me.

"What're you doing back so early?" I asked.

"I just finished with the presentation and they loved it," she said, folding her arms in and taking a bow. "They say, and I quote, 'We wouldn't change a thing,' even though they were looking for something to change. But we both know that they couldn't find something wrong no matter how hard they tried."

"I don't think you'd let them find it," I told her, pulling her up to my step.

"Catherine told me to take the rest of the day off and do whatever I wanted, so I came home to be with you. I thought I might catch you before you . . . You did the laundry?"

"As best I could, but I'm trying to figure out if I like what's going on inside here." I tilted my head toward the town house.

"You won't ever discover anything by standing on the outside looking in. Let's explore."

Namuna grabbed the card out of my hand, put it in the pocket of her Max Mara skirt, then took the lead up the steps into the town house.

"The people sitting on those steps make me ill," I said once we were inside.

"Look, babe," she said brushing her hair behind her ears in one motion. "It is a perfectly gray Saturday afternoon, and we have it together for once. I bet there's wine up there. Don't turn down the pleasures you've put yourself in place to receive. Or, in this case, which have put themselves in front of us to receive. Come on!"

The bricks inside had been exposed to make it "authentic."

Though every one of the five levels had been decorated by different artists, each had the same wine and crackers being served. The first floor's exhibition consisted of checkered tablecloths strewn across the floor for a picnic scene. The artist was serving strawberry jam on little pieces of toast.

The second floor was completely dark, with the only light coming from a source somewhere down the long hallway. In a closet at the end, a peephole revealed a porno looping in a hollowed-out beer keg.

The rooms of the third floor were stacked with old furniture that had been thrown out by the residents of St. Nicholas Place.

On the fourth floor, each of the guests was asked to lie down while the artist drew chalk outlines around their bodies.

"Let's go," I said to Namuna as I pulled myself off the dusty floor. "I can't take it anymore."

"Can we just see what's on the fifth floor?" she said, clearly amused and trying to suppress her laughter. "Maybe everything will come together if we drink enough wine."

I overheard Brenda Hamilton speaking to a large man whose jowls waved each time he brought his Starbucks cup to what I imagined to be his cavity-filled mouth.

"Yes, about nine-fifty for each of the flats, but we'd sell the whole thing for $5.9 million," said Brenda in her best saleswoman's voice.

"Could she be talking about the art?" I whispered to Namuna. "Almost six million for old cat scratching posts and rusted birdcages?"

"We have places all over this area if you're interested," Brenda responded, as her newly French-manicured hand reached smoothly into her Chloé purse to produce a card.

Namuna pulled me upstairs to the fifth floor, and we walked into a cold room with an old baby crib sitting still in the middle. The smile vanished from her face, and the frown that was already on mine became even more pronounced.

Brenda walked in behind us.

"What kind of exhibit is this supposed to be?" I asked.

"My apologies, please excuse this. The fifth floor was to be roped off," she explained, trying to move us out and looking around for somebody who would cordon off the area.

"It's not quite there yet. This belonged to the residents who moved out before we took over. We haven't been able to get the last artist to take it out of here. He insists that the existing crib is art in itself, though I don't really understand what he was getting at."

"How would you?" I answered. "After all, you're just trying to sell this place, right?"

"You will have to leave this room," she said, after brushing the lone wrinkle out of her skirt. "You don't belong up here."

Both of us held our eyes on the crib for as many seconds as we could. Memories rushed into the space around us, but we kept them silent, kept them from each other.

Brenda closed the door behind us, and we walked down the stairs. The sound of the lock that would deny entrance to anyone else echoed behind us.

The thing about working in advertising is that you become skilled at seeing through the curtains others are putting up around you. The real estate company's marketing scheme was to showcase the town house as an art show, attracting people from the lower portion of Manhattan and the booming parts of Brooklyn to see the place under the guise of cheap wine and bad cheese. To tell you the truth, though I was disgusted by the people starting to infiltrate my neighborhood, I was impressed with the plan and wished I'd have thought of it myself.

I felt Namuna's heart sink as she grabbed my hand and led me down the awkwardly spiraling staircase.

"That's what having an open mind does for you," I said, grabbing the cart of clothes we had stowed under the staircase and carrying it down to the street.

"At least now you know what's happening inside," she replied. "It's not always that pretty, but not knowing is worse. Nothing worse than guessing at reality."

Walking back up the block, we passed by a few of the supers who took care of the buildings on St. Nicholas Place, weakened by drink on a Saturday afternoon. How could they get away from the stuff when it had been force-fed into the veins of the block for years?

"You don't have any right to be upset with those people buying up the block," Namuna said.

"I should warn everyone around here what's happening," I said. "The real estate companies are already executing their campaigns. And this is probably just the beginning. It could easily be stopped, or at least we could help the people who live on this block. That way it can stay the same for us. I wouldn't want any part of this walk to ever change."

"Time never stops moving," Namuna said, looking up at the arches that connected the buildings. "What you can control is your present. Our present."

"What the hell can I do?" I asked.

"You can take some of that preaching that you do under your breath and turn it into action. Use that mind of yours for something other than making money."

"Wasn't it money that allowed us to make the move to New York?" I asked.

"It was our desire for something new that opened up the road to New York," she replied.

The neighborhood kids were using the lamppost in front of us as a safe spot in a game of tag. We both stopped and looked back—not at the block, but toward the west—at what we had left behind when we moved here. It was a different life ago.

"I love you," Namuna said. "I will follow you toward whatever dream you want to pursue, but I'm not going to lie to you. There is no such thing as a time machine. We can't erase the past, and I don't want you to waste one moment of your life, of our life, believing that you can."

That was the first time she had mentioned our past since we crossed the George Washington Bridge three years ago. I looked at her, at her stomach, at her eyes. I remembered her waking up crying. I had flashes, the same flashes I had in the dark of night when sleep wouldn't come.

The sounds of the kids playing tag faded in and out as we kissed forever on the sidewalk. The men washing cars with water from the spout on the side of the building went on with their business.

4.

Each building on our block, like pretty much every block in the residential parts of the city, had a different crew standing in front.

The bases of some of the lampposts were unscrewed, with wires sticking out so that a boom box could be hot-wired in, allowing the lyrics to spill out over the static. Rhymes out here were different than they were in California. I guess the people making music here didn't have the luxury of ethereal thoughts—everyone was jammed too close together and just trying to make the next train on time.

We kept moving.

A guy in a van in front of the old castle house—there were, at that time, still a few of those monuments left—sold chicken and rice out of the trunk of his car. Everyone—day laborers, the old drunks, cops, office workers, teachers, mailmen, religious fanatics—stopped to eat there, sitting on the walls of the old Bailey House, whose architecture gave it the appearance of ruling the block. Bellies were being filled all around us. The kids were spilling out to the street. Jump ropes were still in use up here. The arches that capped the buildings were something out of art history books and movie sets.

Everyone was living.

The tree outside of the old Dawn Hotel bloomed pink flowers, as it does once a year. Those days, the Dawn was a home to kids who were no longer kids despite their age. I could see administrators sitting in the windows buried beneath stacks of papers.

On my way to work each day, I would make up little stories about how the people who worked there had a betting pool as to when the flowers would bloom:

"No . . . No. See there. That's still a bud. That's no bloom. Them flowers are blooming when you see petals. I don't see any petals!"

"Right there. Up top, right by the bird feeder. You don't see the petals?"

"I don't see them. Besides, all the flowers have to show petals at the same time or it don't count."

"You crazy."

"Am I? We're all sitting here betting on flowers. Who's crazy?"

I never saw a woman with a baby walk down the steps of her building without someone stopping to help her carry the carriage.

"We should go get a drink at St. Nick's tonight," I said, glancing down the street at the old pub whose sign looked like it had barely survived the winter.

"I would give the least favorite of my toes to redo that whole place. The air even smells in there," Namuna replied. "I'd replace the ceiling and make it so comfortable that people would come from miles around just to indulge in a drink and a set of music."

When Namuna looked at something she wanted to redo, her eyes drifted, as if they were penetrating the walls like a wrecking ball.

"If you did that, if you changed any of it, we wouldn't be able to afford a drink there anymore."

"The point is that the ones who owned it would be doing better. Isn't that of the greater importance? Besides, if I redid the place, don't you think they'd let us drink for free?"

"How'd you get so smart?"

"I happened to marry the right person."

We kept moving.

The Jamaicans, who all lived in the same building and stood on three squares of cement in front of it, were going on about something. I could never understand a word of what they were saying when they spoke to each other. I suppose if I took the time to stop moving, I might have been able to get it. I could tell they were talking about some guy and the money this or that, and that they would never do " 'uch a 'ting!" but that was about it.

The woman I'd been talking to at the Laundromat disappeared into the vestibule before I had a chance to say hello. Two teenagers, the same two kids every day, played chess while their crew kept eyes on the business around them. In the winter, they would bundle up in puffy jackets and knit beanies, and in the warmer months, their games would get longer and their gear become oversize white tees and jeans.

In front of us, Crossing Guard Lita walked her usual route, wearing her orange vest and holding the leashes of her two Dobermans in one hand and an aluminum bat in the other. She had been a crossing guard for twenty years at the school up on 155th until it was determined that she was no longer a necessary expense. Now she worked at the unemployment office processing claims when they needed her, but couldn't let go of her uniform from the job that had defined her.

Finally, we crossed 153rd onto our piece of St. Nicholas Place.

These buildings looked like the movie sets I'd worked on in high school, doing catering gigs on the Warner Brothers lot back in Los Angeles before I started going into offices. The sets showed only the facade of what was, while these buildings spilled life out into the streets as the heat intensified.

The Bodega across the street from our building was in full motion. Women who waited all winter long to get out their lawn chairs had staked their spots and laid their claims. They got larger each year—both in individual size and as a group.

Most prominent on the block was *him*. I had no idea of his name as we had never talked directly, but I assumed it was Edwardo because the awning above the Bodega read EDWARDO DELI. He and his crew smoked and drank all night long. These were the role models for the kids who rode bikes up and down the block. By the time the morning came, trash from the night before marked their spot.

Our apartment building didn't have a stoop. The entryway was a narrow space that separated the building into two sections like a canyon, and when he would blast his music it would bounce around among the bricks and dive right into our place. Man, I hated it. I blamed him and him alone for disturbing what would have been, what should have been, my peace.

An old American flag hung over the entrance to the vestibule that led to our building.

There was a little red door where our super, Armando (who also took care of two other buildings), lived with his family. They were always coming in and out but never let the door stay open for too long. I tried many times to get a glimpse of where they lived, but the apartment itself didn't lie immediately behind the red door. There was a long hallway that led to the actual entrance, and that hallway was all that I ever saw.

We both looked down at whatever kids were sitting on the steps as we moved past them. Namuna's gaze rested on them just a little longer than mine. A girl wearing her Sunday dress on a Saturday held the door open for us.

As always, the inside of the building smelled like a combination of whatever was being cooked in any of the forty-two kitchens. Sometimes we got lucky and biscuits were being baked, but on that day, lard was heavy in the air.

I reached for my keys but realized that I had left them inside.

"You have your keys?" I asked.

"In my bag at the office," she said. "I figured you'd be home. We can get in from the fire escape. Knock on Sukal's door and see if she's there."

Our window shared a fire escape with our neighbor, Sukal Jennings. We had only met her in passing on the stairways or when she was opening her door late at night.

I remember feeling her looking through the peephole when we knocked.

"We're your neighbors next door in forty-two," I said calmly. "We locked ourselves out."

"Sure . . . sure. You're that nice man who helped me up the stairs with my cart. Hold on just a minute and I'll get myself decent."

The chains and locks started to come undone before the heavy door opened. She stood in the doorway, smiling, as if she had been waiting for someone to knock for a long time. She was holding a letter about ten pages deep addressed from the company that owned our building.

"Do you think there's any way we could use your fire escape to get into our place?" I asked.

"Well sure, I'd have to go about moving some of these things out of your way. I haven't used that window in a long time, but I suppose you could. Come on in. Neighbors should be good to each other."

Hers was the only other apartment we had been inside since we moved into the building. Red carpeting covered her hardwood floors and stretched through the entire place. The apartment's layout was the same as ours, only everything was backward—well, not backward for her.

"Do you need something to drink?" she asked. "Hungry?"

"No, we're fine. Just need to get into the apartment," I said.

"Thank you, though," Namuna added, looking at me in disbelief. "That was very kind of you to ask."

"Well, you never know how long these little emergencies are going to take," she said, adjusting her wig. "I just have so many things in here that need clearing away, but I need a break from this darn letter. Just gets more disturbing with each line I try to read. How can they raise my rent that much? Well, I'm not looking for an answer from you, so come on in and make yourself as comfortable as you like."

Photographs and old calendars saved for their pictures hung neatly on the walls of the hallway. They were all of Harlem how it used to be. The block that I had walked down a thousand times looked like another world in Sukal's place. Awnings covered each doorway, and all the men in the pictures wore suits.

"My name is Sukal," she said, smiling softly. "Just in case you're feeling embarrassed about forgetting."

"I didn't forget," I told her. "I just wasn't sure how to pronounce it, and I didn't want to make a mistake and embarrass myself."

"That should never stop you from doing anything."

She noticed me looking at her wall.

"Yes, I knew all of those people and places. We used to go out to all of them, me and Robert, we used to go. Robert is my husband," she said, looking over the timeline of images, punctuated by a clock that bore the name of the bank that must have given it away.

"He's not with me anymore, not for a few years now. Still my husband though."

She moved us into the living room, intent on giving a tour, but slowed down toward the back room, where a window led to the fire escape that we shared. There was no rush for her. An old piano that was used as a mantel held up undusted pictures of her husband and children.

"They're all gone now as well. Not *gone* gone, but not living here anymore. They come around when they can, but it's not enough for me. You sure you don't need something to drink? No? Let me just see if I can't get some of this here mess out of the way for you."

Her window to the fire escape was in a living room that faced the same street I looked out onto each morning, but just a little to the north. I was amazed at how my perspective of the world changed just by looking out someone else's window.

Out of the corner of my eye I could see a huge green chair strewn with cat toys. On the coffee table there was a picture of a big, orange tabby in a special cat frame. I nudged Namuna and she nudged me back, nodding at the cat memorabilia scattered throughout the room.

"I see you looking at Charlie over there," Sukal said, moving the plants that covered the window so we could climb out to the fire escape. "I'm just in love with cats. I had him for the better part of fourteen years, but I'm afraid he's not with me anymore either."

She paused, looking out at the fire escape before she took the last of the wilted plants down. She struggled to open the window and only succeeded in cracking it a few inches wide. Namuna stepped in front of me and made more empty space without asking if she could, opened the window the rest of the way, and went out.

Sukal put her hand on my shoulder, then perched on the arm of the green chair. Namuna looked back in from the fire escape before sliding over to our window.

"The window's closed on our side," her voice reported a few seconds later. "I'm going to have to break in."

"You know, I haven't had that window open for years," Sukal said, drinking in the breeze from outside. "My Robert used to sit out there with his typewriter and work until the sky was at its blackest. Oh, I would try and stay awake with him. I'd bring him his drinks and sit down right here." She moved her hand gently just above the seat of the chair, like a child in a museum who knows she can't touch the painting in front of her but very much wants to.

"I'd read the whole newspaper and just listen to him type away. You know, back then, the neighborhood wasn't like this. It was much rougher. It wasn't the place you see today. I don't really think you'd've been able to walk around here safe. Oh, but I miss those nights up here with him. I miss the sound of his typewriter. It's hard when the one you love is gone. After the funeral, people come by to make sure you're doing fine for awhile, but then go back to their lives and you just get used to living alone.

"Why, I remember shortly after he died, I was in the market, and it wasn't until I was getting that big can of Chock full o'Nuts that I realized I'd been shopping for the two of us. Looking down at that cart full of all his favorite foods, why, I just ran out of there. People must have thought I was a mess. You must think I'm a mess for drifting off into this story. I guess the window being open brought a lot of it back."

"Does it bother you to talk about it?" I asked her.

"No, honey, it feels good. Like holding his hand again."

"What kind of writer was he? Did he write stories?"

"No, he wasn't anything like that. I mean, he knew all those great writers in the neighborhood. I remember that man Langston Hughes—he would come around here and they would go down to St. Nick's for a drink now and then. Back in my day it was called Lucky's. There were so many of those wonderful novelists and poets walking the neighborhood back then. Oh, Harlem was an amazing place for sure. But, no, no . . . Robert wasn't one of the artists. He was a man of science. A man of theory. Though I believe he did see the art in those things."

"So he was just writing for fun all that time on the fire escape?"

She laughed the laugh of a woman who had just caught someone misunderstanding her man.

"Oh no, he never wrote for fun, honey, he wrote to get his thoughts out—when he had the time, that is. All of his theories about this and that—I really didn't understand most of it. Any of it, really. But it was all in his head, and thoughts are no good to the rest of the world if they're stuck in one man's head. What about you?"

"What about me what?" I asked, startled, not ready to be looped into the conversation.

"Well, what is it that you do, other than wait inside old widows' apartments while their wives try to open a window?"

Her words reminded me to check on Namuna.

"You okay out there, Boo?" I said, sticking my head out.

"Don't worry. I almost have it open. I'll come around and knock on her door when I'm through. *Maybe* you can come in."

"I hope so," I laughed.

Sukal smiled at the intimacy of our words, but I could tell that if she had any tears left, she probably would have cried.

I returned to our conversation.

"Me, I'm a copywriter downtown."

"Oh, a writer! How exciting."

"No, not a writer, a *copy*writer. I don't trick myself into believing it's something other than it is."

"You don't seem too happy about what you're doing. Life's hardly long enough to spend time not liking what you do."

"Well, I need to pay the rent and stack cash. People write checks for perfume ads and airline promotions."

"Have you ever tried writing what you like?" she ventured. "You might just be surprised. The money will follow. But even if it doesn't, life will be better if you enjoy yourself as much as you can. My Robert, he just loved what he did, even though he didn't have too much time for it. He was on the verge of a huge breakthrough before he passed. He worked with his hands—in construction, my Robert—but he had a mind for physics. Just never had the opportunity."

The doorbell rang. Namuna had gotten in.

"Well, we'll just have to continue this at another time," Sukal said, as she walked me back down the hallway toward the door. "I hope you'll find time to come back and chat with me. Most people say they are going to, but they never do. See that? The kitchen there—I made it into a sewing room. Robert did most of the work, really, I've just continued on. I made most of those little pillows you see around the house."

I wished that the hallway had stretched for miles so I could hear more. Talking with her was more enlightening than any exchange I'd had in the office since I started working there.

She opened the door, revealing my wife, standing oddly in front of the life we were constructing for ourselves. The next moment, our cat raced out from the half-open door to our apartment. Sukal's face lit up when he darted into hers.

"Oh, look at that little man. He's just beautiful," she said, smiling as Knight ran into the kitchen, then stuck his head out from the doorway.

"He's always trying to escape," Namuna said, brushing the dirt off her hands. "I guess he finally saw his chance and took it."

With the three of us in pursuit, Knight flew into Sukal's living room and nestled himself on the green chair, effortlessly comfortable and gazing lazily out the window toward the fire escape.

"Well how about that," exhaled Sukal. "You know, my Robert used to look across at the other buildings just before he went outside to work. Of course, the streets were quieter back then. You'd hear music, but only the hint of it. People had more sense, I suppose. More love for each other. We were all in the life together. Now we just seem to be fighting for our little piece. He would tell me that he liked to see what everyone was doing, watch their movements, before he started on his work."

"That's a precious memory," Namuna replied, reaching for Knight, who almost took her hand off with a swipe.

"It is, though the reality of the situation is that there were a bunch of young girls across the way just out of school who were sharing an apartment, and they liked to walk around in their skivvies. Men are the same regardless of the era, honey."

Knight didn't protest when Sukal sat in the chair and lifted him onto her lap. She knew the exact place behind his ears to scratch. I could swear a smile broke across his face.

"Do you think I might be able to spend some time with this little man, you know, when you go out? He might get lonely when he's home alone. I know I do."

"I think Knight could use the company anyway," Namuna said. "Why don't you spend the evening with him? It's the least we could do after you opened your home to us. Besides, I'm exhausted and need a nap myself. You can bring him back when you feel like it."

"Well, I won't rush. I'll treat him like my own." She was smiling from deep inside, no longer lost in memory but looking forward to the immediate future she'd be spending with Knight.

After a brief exchange of instructions and reassurances regarding Knight, we left Sukal's red-carpeted apartment and returned to what we knew. Namuna had been up all night perfecting the floor plans for a new penthouse apartment with views of both rivers somewhere on the southern part of the island.

She collapsed onto our bed seconds after we went inside the apartment.

I covered the parts of her she left uncovered.

I still had the smell of Sukal's apartment in my nose. Her description of the neighborhood in her day, and the image of her husband trying his hardest to leave his mark on the world while still supporting a family, made me worry that I'd given up my dreams too easily for the safety of a weekly paycheck. I remember thinking that years of sitting on my balls had perhaps affected their usefulness.

Right then, during a brief moment of nothing moving, I started to think about what I really wanted.

Namuna fell into a deep sleep. I always wondered if she was haunted by the same ghosts that followed me around. If so, they were deep inside of her, well hidden from the world—and from me.

I opened the door to the apartment and closed it quietly after a backward glance to see her lying still, asleep. Down the stairs, then down the block, I made my way toward St. Nick's Pub, where I hoped to get lost in the stories of others and forget about my present, if only for awhile. I felt all of New York exhale deeply and fall into the shadows of the lampposts.

CHAPTER 2

ST. NICK'S PUB

1

Crossing Guard Lita stood smoking, not quite underneath the dark red awning above the entrance to St. Nick's Pub. I got along well enough with her, though it was never clear if she remembered me. The band could be heard warming up inside.

"Hey, Miss Lita, how are the boys this evening?" I asked, bending down to give the two Dobermans a pet.

"They'd be a lot better without this trash all around their feet," she said, putting the smoke out on the tip of her bat and placing the extinguished butt in the pocket of her bright orange vest.

"Well, if you keep talking to enough people," I said, "they might do something about it."

"Why don't *you* go on and do something about it," she said, then disappeared across the street with her hounds.

Now Lita's words joined Sukal's in my head, battling with increasing strength against the voices of reason that kept me plugged into the computer at my office.

My mind flashed back to Sukal's old photos of the block, drifting to imagined pictures of how it had been even before then, when the natives—the true natives—lived here.

History unfolded in my head. The smell of fish and chips from Devin's hung in the air.

I think the first piece of trash I picked up was the plastic wrapper from a pack of cigarettes. Second was a cookie package. Next a juice box. Then an empty can of soda. I couldn't stop. I kept going, not conscious of anything above or around me, only the cleaning of the sidewalk under my feet.

A tray of chicken bones and half-eaten coleslaw lay in front of me—however in the moment I was, there was no way I was picking up that mess with my bare hands.

One block over, just next to the entrance to the 145th Street subway, a new store had opened called HARLEM 99 CENTS. Inside, the kids browsed and bought what amounted to multicolored bags of sugar. The bottles of soda were warm but cheap. Outside, I was picking up the remnants of what was being sold in there. The man behind the counter sat on a high stool.

The store was small and made good use of its space, stacking things so high that if you didn't look close, you'd have no idea what color the walls were. Without too much trouble, I found a broom, a dustpan with a long handle, and a box of garbage bags. I brought them to the counter, put them down, and paid my three dollars. While I waited for my change I had a few seconds to look around—there were TV antennas, bungee cords, wires, and adapters for obsolete electronics. The register jingled shut and the man handed over the change without looking at me.

I was back on the block with a broom and a sense of purpose.

Having spent so much time staring at a computer screen, it was a relief to have a physical connection to the tool I was using. When I started sweeping french fry containers and greased pizza plates out of the gutters, people started watching but clearly felt no obligation to join me. To them, I was just another New York fanatic, like Crossing Guard Lita, who was currently glaring at me from the sidewalk, tapping her bat on the concrete.

"You're not getting paid to do any of this, are you?" she said loud enough so that the kids at the nearby bus stop clowning me and throwing packets of ketchup on the ground could hear.

"No, ma'am," I replied. Something about being around people with gray hair and long lines in their faces brought out an unusual sense of decorum in me. "Just, you know, felt like having a clean block and didn't see the use of waiting for somebody else to do it. I mean, look at all of this."

"Hear that? This boy right here is talking to *you* fools," she yelled. "This boy right here has been in this neighborhood—" she glanced back at me. "How long you been here?"

"About two years, ma'am," I replied, sweeping the broken glass of a beer bottle and dumping the shards into a trash bag.

"Two years! You all been raised here, and you just live in this shit like it's supposed to be that way. You all just blind to what's around you. Why you think these buildings ain't worth the shit that comes out my dog's ass?"

A kid wearing a green fitted Yankees hat stood up tall, flipping the hood of his sweatshirt over the back third of the lid.

"Ain't never gonna be worth nothing, so who cares, you crazy old dog woman?" he said, slapping high fives with his crew. "This is our block. We're gonna keep it like we want. Fuck the rest!"

He took a piece of gum out of its package and tossed the wrapper to the ground. Crossing Guard Lita held her dogs back and tried to figure out if she was more angry or sad.

"You all a bunch of fools!" she yelled. "Don't you know that the more trash you throw on the ground, the less this block is going to be worth? You ignorant asses know what happens after that? People are going to come in here and buy these buildings real, *real* cheap, raise the rent, kick you out, hire you to clean up the trash, fire you from that job, and rent the places out at triple the price. Now then, where you going to go after that? Where are they going to push you after that?"

"Ain't nobody going to push me off *my* block!" the younger

brother of the Green Fitted Hat Kid said. "I'll come out blazing!"

"*Whose* block?" Crossing Guard Lita said, stepping forward. "This ain't your block! You *pay* to *live* here, not to *own* it. You can be moved at any moment. Who's going to protect you? You think someone's going to watch a news story about your sorry selves and want to help keep you on this block? Hell no! People watch stories about genocide every day on the TV, and they just flip the channel to the damn baseball game and forget about it. They just going to flip the channel and forget about you."

She took a deep breath and blew it out into the beginning of the late-night breeze. As if on cue, like a sound editor was poised atop one of the buildings, a trumpet blew from inside the bar. The set was starting at St. Nick's. The sun was nearly down, leaving only an orange glow, then nothing. Outside St. Nick's Pub, the kids moved in from the bus stop, leaned up against the wall and rolled blunts, tossing the excess tobacco onto the street.

Cats rolled up to the curb, creeping between the wheels of parked cars, trying not to get their paws wet from the water spilling from the car wash. The birds stayed in the trees and on the wires, unaffected by what was happening on the block below. I continued my sweeping and cleaning, picking up some soggy reelection flyers from Councilman Macon.

A saxophone had joined the trumpet. I leaned the broom and dustpan up against the wooden wall of the pub and walked down the little jumps of stairs that led inside. I always walked slowly into St. Nick's because it allowed me to feel the footsteps of everyone who had walked in before me.

The ceiling was low. St. Nick's was originally the basement of the building above it. Red Christmas lights were strung along the tops of musty plaster walls that barely held the place up. Pictures torn from magazines were thumbtacked to the plaster. The lights had to be dim. A few tables along the wall were available for a cover charge, but to really see the place, the bar was the best vantage point.

A section of tables was roped off in the front of the band, whose centerpiece was dressed head to toe in snakeskin—snake shoes, snake pants, snake jacket, snake hat with a greasy Jheri curl underneath, the odor of which became more obvious the more he sweated. There wasn't even room enough for the fried fish fumes to make their way in the door.

A slender young man, who was wearing a suit despite the heat, was the owner of the trumpet. That was Granderson Daniels, the grandson of the Bartender. I had talked to him a few times after his sets, but he was always either on his way to school or off to study what he had just learned. The trumpet was a family tradition and a way for father and son to spend time together. That's the thing about living around here—the stories of the people whom you pass by each day start to become your own history. Becoming part of the neighborhood means knowing nicknames and the reasons people hang out where they do.

I glanced over the cast of characters at the bar and noticed Armando, the super from my building, looking down at his bottle of beer. He seemed a different person in his going-out clothes, including a gold medallion that hung to where his thrice unbuttoned shirt created a deep *V*.

"Hey, Armando, I didn't know you came here," I said, sitting down next to him and trying to get the attention of the Bartender, who was trying not to notice me.

"Yes, yes. For years I've been coming, but not in so long," he said. "Before there were too many people even in here I've been coming here. I work in two other buildings, you know. But today, I took off early because it's no good to work *too* much. A lot, it's okay. But *too* much is no good."

Armando relaxed in the lack of light of St. Nick's. Amazing to me that a man could work so hard doing what he did, take care of all the people in those buildings—plus the wife and the kids lurking down that hallway—and still find time to enjoy himself.

"How do you do it?" I asked.

"Do I do what?"

"How do you work so much and still stay positive all the time?"

He took a long drink from his beer and placed it slowly back on same spot from which he'd lifted it.

"You know, you just have to keep going in life. Now . . . " He looked around to see if anyone was listening. "Now, I believe in God, okay? Don't think I don't believe it in Jesus. But, you know, you can make what you want for your life. You can do it like you want to do it. For me, I work, but I still have the life I want. I just don't have it like, like the pictures in the magazine because I made myself not want it that life. I want it my life—my wife's sex, I like it. I like the smell of it, so I have that a lot. I like it my family, a big family, so I have that. I have this block that I have lived on for twenty years. I've seen it all here and will see more. You just have to keep going and not let someone else decide for you."

The music started to pull on the minds of everyone there.

A Japanese man in a casual suit walked in, leading a group of about fifteen tourists, all Japanese also, I assumed, into St. Nick's. The roped-off tables had been set aside for them. All of them were women, around forty years old. The smell of new leather handbags mixed with that of their perfume and makeup. The music never stopped, but heads turned as they filed in.

Armando saw some people he knew and started speaking even more freely, but in his language this time, so I faded away from that conversation. The tourists were all looking around as if they'd been lied to on the brochure. It was not the Cotton Club. I imagined that they were lonely because their husbands had taken them to New York on business but were too busy to spend any time with them. The tour guide came up to the bar to place an order.

He stood tall, readying himself to speak.

"Good evening to you, Yaz," the Bartender said. "Good to have you back."

"Very good to be back, Simon," he said. "How is your son doing?"

"You can hear for yourself, can't you?"

"I was talking more about away from the stage. When he's done, he should come over to Japan. We value hardworking men with good minds over there."

"Yaz, buddy, nobody needs good men with good minds more than we do here."

"Well, then, I'll just have to start spending more time here," Yaz said, laughing. "Anyways, thirty beers, please. Yes, thirty shots of whiskey, please. Thank you."

"I know. I remember," the Bartender said, moving mechanically to fill the order.

"Is this some type of tour group?" I asked.

"Yes, it is something like that," Yaz said winking at me. "This is the Japanese Women's Liberation Group. Good group."

"Liberation? Is it a political group—some part of a church?"

"Church? No. No church. Not for these women. Not anymore I believe. This is liberation group."

"What are they seeking liberation from?"

"Their husbands. Well, they have liberation from husbands, but this is a trip to celebrate it. Here, have a card."

As the Bartender placed thirty glasses and a large bottle of whiskey on the bar for Yaz, I took the card.

"Go on over to your table," the Bartender said. "I'll have someone bring your beer before you get those all poured in."

"Thank you. You two, you come in and join us after we have first round, okay?"

He went back to the table with the bottle of Johnnie Walker Blue. I looked down at the card. He was the president of a group called

32

Japanese Women's Liberation Club, with a tagline that read:

HELPING YOU TO LEAVE HUSBAND BEHIND.

The Bartender shook his head and smiled.

"Man, this guy is in here every month with a fresh batch. Damn divorce rate in Japan is nearly as high as it is here."

"You mean all those women are divorced?" I asked.

"Yeah, man! These women are making mad cash over there, so they're leaving their husbands at a crazy rate. That man right there, he goes and organizes tours for them to "liberate themselves" in America. Myself, I've helped to liberate about five of them this season alone. Doing my part, if you catch me. The world is changing, man. The time when we dominate the whole picture is over. Funny thing is that most men don't know it yet."

"You mind if I bring these to the table?" I asked.

"Ah, I see you want to help in the cause. Go ahead."

I brought the beers to the table and saw the faces of the women. All of them gone from their husbands and traveling across the ocean to Harlem looking for a little peace. The makeup that held their faces together was a little more transparent up close—they weren't as flawless as they'd first appeared. They seemed to enjoy being served. I looked over at Yaz and felt for a moment that he was the luckiest man on the planet. I mean, he was making serious cash and spent his time traveling around with all of these women.

"Thank you for your help, please sit for beer and a shot. Please."

Perhaps I had been looking for the invitation the whole time but was not honest enough with myself to know it. The music was intense at this point. The guitarist's hair juice was dripping heavily down behind his black sunglasses. I sat down between two women, grabbed a beer, and lost myself in the music.

Before his solo, Granderson looked at me with a hint of recognition but no real interest.

One of the women's hands was on my leg halfway through my beer. I looked over at the hand's owner. She neither moved nor acknowledged me, but focused only on my wedding ring.

"You are not yet liberated?" she asked.

"I don't want to be liberated. I'm in love with my wife," I said, not moving her hand from my leg.

"You think that love matters?" she went on, emptying her shot and calling for another one with her free hand while watching the band wailing away. "I'm just speaking of liberation."

The lines carved in her face and the pain hammered in her eyes seemed to move down over the rest of her body, and her Koko Beall suit—not to mention whatever she had on underneath to hourglass her out and drop a few years in the name of freedom—started to show.

"If you like, we could go in back for a little while and test your love for your wife."

"Your English is pretty good," I said.

"That's part of the whole program. We practice before we take this trip. This is like graduation."

She looked me in the eyes for the first time. Her vulnerability struck me motionless. Her hand was moving up my leg. It was the first touch of another woman since I got married. Sure, there had been prolonged leans in the subways from time to time, but nothing as direct as this. I had no intention of taking it any further but didn't move away until a bottle flew over my head, smashing against the wall about a foot away from me.

It was Namuna, who had come down to listen to the set. She stormed out of the place, and I bolted out of my chair after her. My stomach was hollow as I chased her.

Namuna was flying up the block. I caught up to her in the small park in the middle of the street. The kids who had been up against the wall of the pub were now sitting in the middle of the island park. They were in the midst of their own conversations but stopped to check out the drama about to unfold. "That's what my eyes have to see?! I come down here to surprise you and *that's* what is waiting for me?" Namuna boomed.

"I didn't do anything. *She* had her hand on me. Hey, slow down!"

Namuna had taken off again, and I stood there for a second before following her.

"Yeah, you best get after her," the Green Fitted Hat Kid said. "And pick up my shit if you have time!" Everyone busted out laughing.

As I ran after Namuna, the old men on the stoops around the block were looking at me and smiling—were they laughing at me, or reflecting on moments when they themselves chased women they'd made angry down the block? In blocks and dirt roads all over the world, probably at that very moment, men were running after women trying to erase some wrong they had done.

The alcohol evaporated and my stomach was aching for food. I finally caught up to her in front of the Bodega, where the crew had their full drunk on and the women had seemed to forget about the strollers that had been sitting there for far too long. The radio blasted a terrible soundtrack as Namuna crossed the street without looking, barely avoiding a gypsy cab that was looking for help to make the rent that night.

"Are you going to slow down enough to talk?" I yelled, crossing after her, more cautiously than she had.

"For what? What you truly desire is back there. She's waiting for you, I'm sure."

"What I want is right there in that apartment. In the place we built together."

"You didn't build anything. I'm going to tear it apart when I get upstairs."

"Come on, Boo, I—"

"Don't call me that. Don't use nicknames on me. Don't use *any-thing* on me. This is bullshit! I never believed anything you said anyways."

She found her key and headed through the door.

"Don't follow me up. You don't deserve to be upstairs with me tonight. You should be on the street with the rest of these fucking cats and dogs who don't have a home—just looking for some warm body to crawl up inside of."

"I love you," I told her.

"I'm not sure you even know what that means."

I could tell those words hurt her more than they did me. She didn't mean it, but she felt it, and that was enough. She went inside, leaving me on the block.

I couldn't follow her. She didn't look back on her way up the stairs. I wanted so badly to go with her but didn't. There was no movement in my legs. I finally coaxed them to amble up to the top of the block, where 155th met St. Nicholas Place. The Macombs Dam Bridge stretched out from there, over the Harlem River and into the Bronx; the view of Yankee Stadium and the one under construction to take its place was split by the housing projects. A game was going on. On the bridge, kids were moving across to the Bronx—not to the game, but to their homes.

I remember a sporadic stream of people moving on the bridge toward the stadiums. To me, the two were heaven and hell. The old one was still lit up and home to twenty-six championships and legends who ruled the city, and the new one was being constructed out of the money that those legends helped create.

Cars flew by the people on the bridge. The river below looked like thick cement that had been poured into a canyon.

I followed across the bridge toward the stadium. Yankee Stadium is on the edge of the Bronx, so walking across the Macombs Dam Bridge, you pass by a set of projects that stand on the footprint of the old Polo Grounds—the place where the baseball Giants played, back when Harlem was how Sukal's old pictures showed it to be. Next you pass by the Rucker, the classic church of street yard ballers.

Instead of watching the game, I headed to River Avenue, better known as Yankee Row, under the tracks of the No. 4 train and adjacent to the stadium. It had pretty much stayed the same since the 1930s, when the stadium was built. Bars and people hawking all things Yankee dominated the scene.

I walked into Yankee Tavern, where the game played on the TV while those around the bar sat glorious in their moments of escape. Investment bankers with their throwback jerseys and off-duty subway conductors talked about math equations in front of black-and-white photographs of baseball players. Those Yankees kept their ghosts working for them. Ruth. Joe D. Mantle. Yogi. Man, these guys never stopped hustling for the pinstripes.

I think men go to these games for some type of connection to a tradition—an attempt to find their place in history. Perhaps that's why I was over there, looking for some way to connect to the past where I would not have made the mistakes I had. Was there some secret here in the Bronx to be found somewhere above the smell of beer and under the rumble of the same conversation that had taken place for years?

All I could think about was Namuna. I drank the rest of a Red Stripe and watched Derek Jeter step up to the plate and take in the flashbulbs that were trying to capture him.

I paid the bartender ten dollars for a five-dollar beer and asked to use the phone. It was one of those old-school jobs with the rotating dials.

"Boo, I'm sorry. You know I didn't do anything."

"I know. It's the almost that I'm worried about. Where are you?"

"I'm watching the Yankee game at a bar in the Bronx. You want to take a cab over here and meet me?"

"No, babe, I'm tired. Just come home when you're finished."

"Is it okay to come home?"

"Always."

"I have this feeling that I have to do something different with my life. The path—this path I started down—it's dominating me. I need to veer off. Whatever direction I go, though, it has to be with you. I know that much."

"You can tell me about it when you come home."

"I love you," I told her.

Jeter sent one over the fence, and the crowd in the bar roared, drowning out whatever response she might have given.

I hung up and looked around at the patrons at the bar, then at the men in frames on the walls looking over them. Thoughts of how I was going to be remembered started to overtake the voices in my head.

CHAPTER 3

THE BRIDGE

1

I always tried hard to come home directly from work and spend as much time as possible with Namuna. I was never one to hang out with coworkers once everything was finished.

The A train during rush hour on any given day would look like this: stressed-out Wall Street folks who still had their ties tied in case there was someone to meet; power women in suits shining out of the crowd, praying silently to find a person brave enough to find out what trouble they went through picking out their underwear; old women who couldn't believe youngsters wouldn't give up a seat for them; Russians on their way to transfer to the E train home to Queens.

Those of us going way uptown had looks of anticipation.

At 59th Street, the subway would empty out a bit because the express run to 125th Street was about to start. People in New York spend a good part of their days thinking and talking about which trains they need to catch. It's unifying and gives us a sense of being experts in something.

A text from Namuna before I went into the station:

Can U PCK Up Sum 'Cense on 125. Luv ya.

So on a hot day in early September, I got off on 125th to get some oils and incense for the apartment. Whenever the seasons changed in our building, a new smell would creep out from the walls and float through our hallways.

When I walked upstairs from the platform I was in the middle of history. One side wall had a picture of Harriet Tubman, already old and finished with her heroic ways, being escorted somewhere. Opposite of that was a panoramic shot of how Harlem once was. Each time I got off at that station I wanted to jump into that black-and-white photograph, but had I tried, I would have just knocked myself unconscious onto the concrete just below the image.

2

One Hundred Twenty-fifth Street was everything that was good about Harlem and everything that was changing about Harlem and everything that had made Harlem what it was.

Street vendors lined the block. Posters of beautiful bodies, bootleg CDs of Sam Cooke, Otis Redding, the O'Jays, Bob Marley, and Malcolm X speeches. There were wooden carts selling organic soaps and oils. Homemade T-shirts with Ali standing over Liston in their second fight, and with Jordan soaring through the universe in the original Bulls uniform and rocking the OG Airs.

The bottles of oil rattled on wooden carts every few feet. It was the same cart over and over again, selling magnificent smells. Next to them were the indie booksellers. Now these people were the heroes I silently admired—they had stayed away from the corporate world but managed to survive within the spectrum of capitalism because they created their own and sold it.

Tour buses crawled up and down the block, moving quickly past the statue of Adam Clayton Powell and stopping in front of the Apollo Theater. The cameras were pulled out and another box in a checklist was ticked off. Across the street, men were selling pictures of lynchings and police dogs attacking citizens. I wondered if some agency would eventually buy ad space on them.

Children of Israel preachers, wearing heavy black robes with silver stars and thick headdresses dripping with sweat, were standing on ladders trying to get people to listen to them about the biblical implications of what was happening, but everyone, including myself, went about their business looking for a deal.

Old newspapers rolled along the sidewalk, telling a story about a recent rezoning program that had been passed. I only caught the headline. Down the side streets, old brownstones that had been recently bought up and rebuilt were redecorated with FOR SALE signs furnished by Brownstone Restoration Properties. I picked up the incense and oils from a cart in front of the Lids store, which was advertising a 30% OFF SALE on throwback merchandise. The best part about making cash was my ability to indulge my wants, which, to be honest, were never of a particularly monetary nature. One of my only material desires was for memorabilia of anything baseball, especially hats. I guess it came from years of being alone with my baseball cards as a child.

The throwback hats were buried deep in the back of the store, so I had to walk past twenty-five different kinds of Yankee bills adorning the walls. I think it's a rite of passage—not to mention part of the city uniform—to have a Yankee hat, but me, I just could never get with it. I mean, I was a baseball purist for sure, but I loved to hate the Yankees—probably because I wasn't part of it. I wasn't a sucker either; I wouldn't jump on board and be part of it just because they were classics. I had left those ghosts in the Bronx for good. At least I thought I had.

A Milwaukee Brewers lid hung on the wall—the one with the old *M* and *B* formed together in the shape of a baseball glove. So cool. No money, earnings, or accomplishments could bring about that feeling. It could only exist in a moment of reflection on my youth. I put the hat on and looked in the mirror, wanting so much to see that little boy who had always desired that piece. In the reflection, though, all I could see were the echoes of those men who rode the D train up to Yankee Stadium each day thinking they could recapture something.

Did it look silly? I looked in the mirror longer and longer, until I could find the angle where I wasn't so much seeing my face as I was seeing the hat and what it represented. Deciding I had to have it, I took it to the register, manned by a kid who wasn't even alive when the Brewers originally wore that style.

"I was thinking about getting that one too. Sick, right?" he said.

"I've wanted one for years," I told him.

"I'd never wait that long for something I wanted," he told me.

I could see the whole world in that face. Working, but without his mind on the shop too much. His T-mobile cell rang the tune of the latest MF Doom beat. "Yup. Off in 25. Tonight's gonna be fire. Okay, then. See you at the spot. Can't wait. *Cannot wait!*"

He handed me the hat in a bag, but I told him there was no need and put it right on my dome. It was almost dark outside by the time I hit 125th again. The stores had started to roll up their metal gates and the street vendors were folding up their tables. Even the Children of Israel guys had lost their voices and were calling it a night.

Outside the Apollo, people were dressed up and ready for Amateur Night inside. I remember telling myself that if I ever learned to do the electric slide, I would probably get onstage there. It was time to head home. True enough, I lived in Harlem, but down here wasn't home.

I decided to take the No. 1 train up Broadway and walk over from 163rd when I got off.

3

The elevated platform of the No. 1 train at 125th Street and Broadway felt like the New York of fantasies, but the backdrop of brick buildings and the hint of sky gave depth to the scene.

The No. 1 train hustled along the tracks. A group of teenagers, heads hung down, wore zip-up hoodies with skeleton bones printed on each side, and skulls on the hoods.

Being underground all the time brought me closer to the rats, which the city was constantly trying to eradicate but couldn't. I had eventually accepted this futility as fact. Taking the train aboveground in New York City made me feel more alive. Below, McDonald's and Burger King pumped slow cancer into the community, though I couldn't preach too much back then, as my job was to help promote those companies.

Hundreds of people living out their lives zoomed by, measured in brief views into windows. Subway prophets talked about how the world was at its breaking point. Timberlands were being worn with shorts. I gave up my seat to a woman old enough to have stories to fill ten books but only time to tell me one of them:

"I took this train with my daddy after he got off work. He used to tell me that the sound the train made going over the tracks was the universe acting as a chorus for the lullaby he was singing to me. That's what he told me he did during the day, that he spent so much time away from me because he had to come up with the perfect song to sing me to sleep. I found out later that he was a security guard downtown. There wasn't much to do so he would just memorize songs to sing me that went along with the sound of the train going over the tracks. I ride the trains to hear those songs."

People came in and out of my life quickly here. Entire pieces of them became stuck to me with each random story.

The train stopped at 158th and Broadway. Though it was night, the street was still filled with leftover rush hour foot traffic. This was Washington Heights. Anything below 155th Street was Harlem.

I walked down Broadway to 155th and made a left at the old Trinity Church graveyard that took up the entire block. This was one of the few cobblestone sidewalks left in this part of town, and it had not been well cared for. The pieces of stone were protruding from their places as if the bodies from the graveyard had found their escape route and needed to make one more push to freedom. If there was any haunting going on in Sugar Hill, the suspects were likely to be housed here.

I yelled out.

"*What am I supposed to be doing with my life?*"

It all seemed to rush in and around me just then. I couldn't sit in an office much longer looking at that little clock at the bottom corner of the computer. There was no amusement in emails and websites—especially closing them quickly when someone walked by even though they were on their way to a desk where the same thing was about to take place.

I didn't expect a response and didn't get one.

"Well, I'm over on St. Nicholas Place if you need me. No rush."

Continuing past the graveyard, I crossed the street and passed by PS 28, whose walls were painted with inspirational figures and colors that made me wish I had taken advantage of school while I was still young.

The old Yankee Stadium stayed lit up at night even after the games had ended. I was about to turn down St. Nicholas Place when I saw a kid with a yellow box of M&M's sitting at the entrance to the bridge.

He looked like he was about to stand and start off toward the Bronx until he noticed me notice him.

"You want to buy some chocolate?" he said as if he had said it thousands of times that day without much of a reaction from anyone.

"Sure," I told him. "Though it might help you sell more if you say the name of the candy you're selling. Customers always identify with a brand."

I pulled out a dollar and got a bag of the peanut M&M's.

"What are you doing out here so late?" I asked.

"I usually stay out until the sun comes up," he said. "Got to see the sun come up over the spot. One day I'll be playing there. Best believe that."

"Your mom lets you stay out till this hour?"

"I can tear up the outfield like Bernie did in the day."

"I didn't think young kids like you knew who he was," I said, opening the iconic yellow wrapper. "He was coming up when I was your age."

"This here is New York. You ain't from here, I can tell, but anyway, this is New York, so we know all our Yanks. I study each swing I see. Never been to a game, but they show them on TV a bunch. Always wanted to go to the stadium though. I'll be playing there one day. My first day in that stadium will be my first game in the majors. Hey, you got one of those Brewers hats on. You from Milwaukee?"

"No, it's a throwback."

"What's a throwback?"

"You telling me you don't know what a throwback is?"

"Whatcha got to be on me like that? Just asking you a question."

He went back to watching the bridge.

"Well, I gotta get back to my wife. Thanks for the candy. See you around, though I hope not this late. You'll be tired for school."

"Being up don't fade me," he said holding his gaze on the stadium. "Besides, staying awake for that school mess isn't all that hard. Usually I'm here just before the sun comes, but something brought me out earlier tonight. Sometimes, you know what I'm saying, you just do things without a good reason."

He looked deep into my eyes as if he was begging me not to answer him but only to understand what he was talking about. The air warmed, I tipped my cap awkwardly to him, and walked down past the fried Chicken and Pizza joint, past the tire shop and the storefront church where the Preacher was working up to his message, until I got back to my building, where the light was on in our fourth-floor window.

The Bodega Guy was chain-smoking and doing his sway-around dance while his buddies bummed smokes off each other. I gave him a look, but that was all. He just kept on motioning to people to move up and down the block.

I walked heavily up the stairs. When I got to the fourth floor, there was a black case sitting in front of our door. Attached to it was a note:

"I'll keep Knight one more day if you don't mind. Here's a thank-you for the company." —Sukal

I lifted the old case and brought it inside. Namuna was in the living room at the end of the hall with her floor plans spread in front of her.

"You're later than usual," she said, not lifting up her head. "I was almost worried."

"I'm good. Just took a different way home. Here are the smells," I said, handing her the bag with incense and oils.

"What's that you're holding?"

"Sukal left it for me—for us, I mean."

"No, I believe that is for you."

"Why do you say that?"

"Women are always leaving you things. It's just . . . it's nothing. She's harmless. What's inside?"

I opened the box and was amazed to see her husband's old type-writer sitting there in front of me. It was perfectly polished, as though the years had never passed. Its keys seemed to call out for my fingers, but I had no idea what to write.

"What am I supposed to do with this?" I asked.

"You're sometimes just a little bit more dense than I thought you were," Namuna said. "When a woman gives you something, there is always a reason or purpose. She wants you to write something other than what you do at work."

"Why would I do that? I'm not that kind of writer."

"Maybe she knows you better than you know yourself. Why don't you try for once to get down what's inside of you? It might help you to empty out your head just a bit. There's no nobility in carrying your past with each step you take."

A woman's understanding of a man.

CHAPTER 4

FIRE ESCAPES

1

Sitting on our fire escape about to hit the keys of that old typewriter felt like being in the novel of a life I had always tried to run away from. I had no idea what to write. I had never just written something without a plan of action, an outline, or a creative brief to get me started. What was I supposed to put down on the blank piece of paper?

On the street across from me, I could see a super using a hose to clean off the stoop where the women had been sitting, and from where they'd failed to picked up their grease-soaked paper plates. He didn't seem to mind, but then again it's tough to get a read on facial expressions from up on a fire escape.

The small park just above the intersection of 155th and St. Nicholas Place had benches where men sat and talked for hours on end. If they were not old in those moments, they would be soon. Across from them, though I couldn't see him, the Kid was waiting for the sun to rise over the stadium. I figured I'd keep pace with him.

A light on in the apartment across from us silhouetted a woman walking back and forth, back and forth. She was shapely, but any female silhouette is shapely at that time of night. She paused for a moment when she realized she was being watched. Even from far away, when a man sees a breast moving in a window, the rest of the world stops. I decided not to look anymore and just continue typing so that she would be the one looking at me. It was more sensual for me to know a half-naked woman across the way was watching me write on a fire escape.

There was never a need for me to hide in the shadows during those early years in Harlem. I peeked into Sukal's window and saw her passed out in the chair with Knight. She had fallen asleep trying to get through that letter from our building's management company. Most of the windows in the building across the street had bedsheets covering them. Namuna had sewn curtains and built custom pelmets for us.

I remember those first keystrokes on the old typewriter. They were the most important words I had ever written. I wrote about the unusual amount of furniture being thrown out on the streets.

"What are people using to sit on at home?" was the first sentence.

The action of making that sentence made me happier than anything I'd ever been paid to write, though I had never written to be happy.

I had enough time to think about the drive across the country that got us here, and about the friendly teenage innkeeper in Kearny, Nebraska, who joined us for breakfast one morning and asked if he should drop out of school and take off across the country. Should he take that chance? Was he still using God as his balancing rod across the tightrope of uncertainty? When we told him that we just packed everything up and headed to New York with nothing but a vision of what we wanted, he looked ready to jump into our dream. He asked about San Francisco. Said that he wanted to give that a try and asked if I had ever lived there.

"Amazing place," I told him. "Went to school out there and learned more on those dark streets than I did in most of those classrooms."

"What about the religion?" he asked. "Is there a foundation for faith?"

"Well, if you don't mind vampires and are very open sexually, you'll be fine."

In his eyes I saw a young boy who had been going to church since he could walk, and I didn't feel like getting too heavy about that stuff over a free continental breakfast. Hell, the kid hadn't even read *On the Road* yet, how was I going to start tearing away at his religion?

Even back then, before we had gotten to Harlem, strangers always seemed to feel at ease opening their souls to me.

I thought about the time we stopped in Iowa and got out at the gas station, and how the people there laughed at us for locking our van door when we went in to pay for gas.

I thought about the folks in the truck stops and detour road towns of Illinois—how they kept themselves warm with huge cups of coffee and even bigger sandwiches stacked with meat. They had no time for fiction but plenty of sports stations on the radio.

The little space up on the fire escape was relaxing. I could see why Sukal's husband would sit out here and work at his dreams after he came home from working at his job. Looking down on the page, I saw that all my thoughts had somehow made it out. The white of the paper was now only a background for the imprints of the keys. There was something magical about how I had the only copy in the world.

2

The sunrises in Harlem use the same star as the rest of the world, but the filter is different.

A couple wearing matching old-school Pumas with fat laces made out against the lamppost before going their opposite ways to school for the day.

The heavy bricks took in much light from the sky, enriching their redness. It was like a switch being turned on, signaling everyone to start moving. A few seagulls who'd lost their way were circling below the departing planes.

There were no saxophones blowing. No soundtrack other than

the keys hitting the page. You could make out lights turning on in the apartments across the street. The girl I had been watching watch me had gone from her window long ago.

Whatever ghosts were around did their best to duck into the shadows, of which there were plenty. The man who opened the Bodega in the mornings unlocked the ice machine outside and rolled up the front gate to start his workday, but not before having something to smoke with his coffee. A large orange cat that had been waiting to start work himself lunged inside to begin mouse patrol.

I could see Armando below, walking outside with a broom and a hose to clean the street.

The always-open tire shop next to us switched shifts—the people coming and going wore the same uniforms. In front of the all-night Chicken and Pizza spot, Chicken Bob, a street cat who pretty much lived in the doorway, made out well chewing on a chicken bone with half the meat left on it. He walked quickly down the block, trying not to draw any notice from the other strays or pigeons who were all looking for something to help make it through their own morning. I needed some coffee myself. I left the typewriter on the fire escape and made my way down the side of the building by way of the rusted iron.

When I reached the final landing, the street was still a story below me, but I jumped anyway, feeling like I was in the middle of fiction that could not be altered by reality.

Chicken Bob hustled past me.

"Morning," I said to the tall man behind the thick protective glass wearing a fitted Reds hat. His rim was not flat like the Green Fitted Hat Kid—he had it bent proper.

"What do you need, sir?" he asked, and the way he used the word "sir" really laid my age on me.

"Same as always. Just a cup of coffee."

He handed me one of those little blue cups that have been used forever in New York. Even if the coffee tasted like crap, the nostalgic image was enough to make the experience pleasurable.

"Fifty cents."

"Yesterday it was seventy-five," I said, not complaining, just a little confused.

"You're going to tell me about my job? You think you know something, huh?"

"Only what I knew yesterday," I told him, handing him the dollar and getting fifty cents in change.

I walked out back onto the block, where I saw the Kid who had been sitting on the bridge now heading up 155th toward Amsterdam. He had no intention of looking back.

Not too far from here, the island was taken from the natives in the greatest used-car swindle of all time. I looked up and saw a hand with a cup of coffee and another smoking a cigarette, hanging out the window of the half-naked girl. The thought of tobacco made me ill, until I realized that it was my contribution to the industry that was actually making me sick. She flicked the butt out the window, thinking she was making the moment something more than it was. It landed ugly on the sidewalk I had cleaned just yesterday.

3

It was around this time I stopped working in offices for good.

We were doing a project for a hotel down in the Dominican Republic that needed a promotional boost to draw folks there on vacation. The creative brief that was put on my desk let me know that we were supposed to highlight the wonders of the Dominican Republic and talk about how it's a magnificent tourist destination full of sandy beaches, scuba diving, five-star hotels, lobsters, and everything else you can't afford in the U.S. but can readily devour down there.

Those deep projects, the ones with a decent amount of research behind them, always allowed me to immerse myself in a world of creativity. With my headphones on, poring through stats, it was easy to create the illusion of being productive.

The more research I did, the more I found out about the Taino, the people who had been living in what is now the Dominican Republic for five thousand years, before the island was "discovered" by Columbus, who immediately asked them to agree to give up their customs, or at least infuse Christianity into each festival or celebration. Of course, if they didn't agree, their women would be raped and the men made into slaves. I guess that when one is at the end of a sword, religion is not such a terrible alternative. Each time I wrote about a golf course, I started imagining the severed head of a Taino rolling around on the green while oblivious travelers stuffed their faces with lobster and tossed the shells at the rolling head.

It turns out that the carnival there, as in other parts of the region, was originally a festival to celebrate the change of seasons. When the Spanish came in, they made it a celebration of Christ. The rich minerals in the region made it impossible for Columbus to leave, and word spread quickly. Soon the French came and took a third of the island, making it what is today Haiti. After a few decades, history fades away, different flags are raised, a new race is created, and resorts are built. I couldn't help thinking that by writing to promote those resorts, I was not only part of the chain of slavery but also a key player in the continuing promotion of it.

It's one thing to sell out so that I can put food on the table. I mean, I did live in America, right? There are enough ghosts here of those we've taken, beaten, enslaved, changed, and remarketed already, no? Until that point, I had justified everything I did by saying that it had been done this way in most countries, but each word I wrote for this hotel campaign felt like piling more riches into Columbus's treasure chest.

I looked at myself through the eyes of the five-year-old I once was. This was me now—zoned in front of a computer producing words that did nothing for the world but made money for people who owned resorts that were built on the bones of slaves.

There was a kickoff meeting in the conference room to bring all of the designers and programmers up to speed on the project. I remember the slow walk down the narrow hallway toward the meeting. Most people's heads hung low, their spines bent into question marks from sitting in office chairs for most of their lives. I started to think that perhaps we were being marched in the same formation the Spanish had driven the Taino.

The conference room was quiet save for the typing sounds of the admin assistants seeping through the door. Nobody was speaking aside from small talk or vanilla jokes. Everyone had a pad with them, ostensibly to take notes on anything important that was said, but that would no doubt stay blank or be doodled on once the meeting was over. We were shown a brief PowerPoint presentation about the island and the features offered by the hotel, but all I kept seeing were bodies being stacked upon one another as building blocks to help construct more resorts.

I could hear each breath taken in the room. Somebody unwrapped a stick of gum and tossed the little piece of paper on the ground. The sounds of the creative director stumbling over her presentation drilled through my head. She was a nervous type who wasn't confident enough in her own creativity to let others show what they could do. It wasn't her fault. Everyone in advertising wants to become the creative director of a company because they imagine there's more artistic control in that position. They soon realize that they have to deal heavily with the administrative side of the company, and that their role is merely a go-between for the suits and the artists.

Nobody much wore suits anymore.

The floor was opened up for ideas. As they started coming in, I heard each one as another scream from the Taino. Looking around to see if anyone else was feeling what was boiling inside me, I had a thought that if I released what was truly inside of me, I could start something remarkable. We could take back the corporate system that would otherwise eventually enslave us all.

I stood up.

"How about we put in some secret code underneath the island? This way, if somebody rolls over a certain location, a burial ground will surface and we could show the bodies and give statistics about everyone who was murdered there. It wouldn't be found easily, of course, but if you happened to be searching for a spa or something and came across it, you might just unlock a secret part of the site. Think of the publicity!"

There was a silence so silent it almost made me long for the sound of the radio blasting from the Bodega. Almost. Nobody wanted to be the first to speak. Perhaps inside one or two bodies around the table, a hint of excitement deep within was pushing them to stand up, but nobody was listening to the little voices inside of them except for me. I smiled.

"Well, I'm sure none of you will say what you want to, but this . . . this is a chance to be great and break ourselves apart from the rest of the agencies doing the same thing we are. If you want to grow, you must be radical. Nothing more radical than telling the truth."

I walked out of the room and took an uncomfortable elevator ride where nobody had anything to say, so they pretended to look at their phones until the doors opened up; I went out onto Broadway and Broome, in the heart of SoHo. Broadway itself had been, a long time ago, the main trail used by the natives who once lived on this island to travel from the tip of Manhattan to the bottom. I looked north and knew that I could walk a straight, continuous path all the way back to Harlem.

I tried for a deep breath of air, but the guys from the Duane Reade drugstore, taking a break from their hourly gigs, were puffing on cigarettes. A pickup truck rolled by, scratched and dented by heavy use and blasting Boogie Down Productions:

"... *broken down to his very last compound, see how it sounds, a little unrational, a lot of emcees like to use the word dramatical. Fresh, for '88 you suckas!*"

The light turned green and the truck pulled away. Had it really been almost twenty years since I first heard KRS-One? I remember pretending to be him, using a turkey baster as a microphone. What happened to that kid?

I went back upstairs, and walking over toward my desk, nobody would look at me. The directors and managers of this and that all stopped talking as soon as I walked in. Nobody would look me in the eyes. When I tried to sit down, I heard the words that everyone hears before they lose their job.

"Can we talk to you for a second?"

I went into some nondescript office where a few little action fig-ures of Jesus and Q-bert that were supposed to be ironic had, over time, turned iconic. "We're going to let you go," the creative director said. "I'm not sure why you said what you said, but this is a profes-sional environment. We have to be professionals here."

I looked back at my desk where the IT guy was fixing my com-puter so I couldn't get on it anymore. It was over for me.

"Thank you," I said to the creative director. "I'm alive again."

She said something out of a managerial manual and turned back to her computer. I walked out of her office and gathered the few books I had in my desk drawer. I started taking down my little pictures but then realized that, wherever I was going next, I didn't want to take the stench of the office with me.

I looked around at everyone, all of whom remained at their desks, and felt a sense of self that I hadn't in a long time. I left the office and the world of corporate America a hero to myself, and for once, that was enough.

I took the road the natives had walked before it was taken from them and headed back uptown.

4

Getting off at 147th and walking back up St. Nicholas Place, I felt the daytime would last forever. I had so much time to think. The street was filthy because the supers only swept in the mornings, leaving the ten percent of the block's population—the ones who didn't care where they tossed their trash—to destroy the visuals for the rest of us.

A young girl wearing her school uniform untucked walked past, listening to her Walkman. She flipped the tape over as she strolled by. That was the first time I'd seen someone with a tape—an actual tape—in a long time. The same group of kids who had been mocking me when I was cleaning up earlier had finished watching the girl walk by and resumed nodding their heads to the huge radio plugged into the lamppost from which hung Councilman Macon's newest campaign poster.

It was a clean picture of his face with the words RACISM ENDS WITH YOU across the bottom.

Little red and green lights darted across the equalizer of the radio.

"Grand Verbalizer, what time is it?"

The sound of X Clan is one that you know right away. These kids probably weren't even born when X Clan first dropped, and here they were banging an old-school blaster plugged into a lamppost up in Harlem, listening to what I was listening to when I was their age.

"Deeper than the seafloor traveled by the mantis. You copycats will never know, for you the funk will never flow."

When X Clan first came out, the last golden age in hip-hop was about to start. It was still about consciousness back then. Guns were the reality and music was the escape. I walked by the kids and back up the block to my apartment building, the sounds of my youth going off all around me.

I think that for those of us who grew up without a father around, hip-hop provided the male voice that guided us into adulthood. I was lucky to have had the teachers I did, kicking knowledge through rhyme. Had I not had Chuck D telling me the truth, I might have walked through life much more ignorant than I was.

I remember being hired out one time to create copy for a few of these artists who did nothing but talk about money, guns, and bitches. This was early in my career—the company that hired me knew I loved hip-hop and played on that. They asked me what I thought would really hurt the rap industry so they could avoid it. I told them. I told them that rap music was on the verge of completing the revolution that the Panthers had started and Reagan had unsuccessfully tried to kill. I told them the only thing we had to avoid was showing money and jewelry as symbols of achievement instead of consciousness. They told me I was going to be responsible for preserving the foundation of the movement.

I had no idea they were picking my brain and using what I told them to create MCs that would infiltrate the industry, but I was still guilty because I didn't walk away when I found out. By then I had already bought my mother a house and told her she could retire after twenty-five years of teaching. No excuse though—just the facts.

Armando was in front of my building, just coming back from the one he took care of around the corner. He noticed me and smiled.

"You home early today."

"I lost my job."

"Oh, man. Sorry about that. You'll be good though. The life, it is long."

"I'm not worried," I told him.

"You must have it a lot of money then. Me, I cannot lose my job."

One of his kids came out of the little red door to the hallway that led into his apartment and headed up the block.

"You want to come in and have a drink? You feel better after you do."

"I don't really feel all that bad now," I told him. "But I'd love to come in for a drink."

He opened the entrance and ducked down inside. I followed him past the unspectacular, uneven white walls. It was just as I had imagined it to be, until we reached a mahogany door with a truly vintage brass handle.

"From now on, what you see is what I made myself. This door it took me two years to complete. Beautiful." He rubbed it like a man rubs the shoulder of his sleeping wife late at night. He slowly opened the door that led to another long, deep hallway, all done in dark wood grains. Pictures showing generations of his family were encased in gold frames along the walls. He walked slow so that I would walk slow through his world.

"All of this I made."

"Amazing," I said.

"No, not amazing. Just make it. You too. You can do it."

"I don't have time to do anything like this, even if I could."

He stopped underneath a fading picture of a woman surrounded by six kids.

"You know, we all have the same time in one day. What you do with it is the only thing different about us. Don't believe what anyone tells you is impossible. You should listen to the man who controls your heat and water, no?"

He continued his slow roll.

"Who are you really, Armando?" I asked.

"I am the man who makes this whole building go. Right? Am I not one of the most important people in your life then?"

"I guess so."

"And you've never even been down here. You just call when

something is wrong, right? To clean it up the toilet or fix it the door. You never just call to say hello."

"I don't know you that well," I told him.

"That's how you get to know people, my friend."

We moved through the belly of the building, and I could feel the weight of all of the other floors stacked one upon another above us.

Another door opened, and he led me deeper inside his underground, hand-carved, customized apartment. Echoes of our footsteps were the only sounds to be heard.

"No music from the streets down here," he said, as if he read my mind. "Do you like the table? I made that. Cut it out of a fallen tree from the park above the block long time ago."

He grabbed a remote and turned on some Ornette Coleman to play lightly under the conversation we were about to have. He moved over to a liquor cart and poured us two glasses of Dalmore Scotch. Handing me a glass, he started in, sitting down on his leather sofa.

"You didn't kill a cow to make that, did you?"

"You know, my friend—"He paused to take a sip. "Ah. You see, this makes all of those hours of work doable. Anyhow, yes, you see, I can tell maybe you are one of those people who looks for reasons to be unhappy. You find it fault in those around you so you cannot see your own."

"I just see things that way," I told him. "I've been trained to home in on people's weaknesses so I can find out how to make them happy."

"Perhaps the problem is, you go digging through history trying to find reason for unhappiness when there is none. There is only—what is it my daughter was studying? 'The course of human events.'"

We both drank for a moment, and then a moment more.

"I can't just look away when something is wrong," I said. "It's not in me anymore."

"There is nothing worse than turning away from something that is wrong. However, if you constantly go *looking* for something that is wrong, you will find yourself in the dark places. The problem with that is in the dark, you never see it clearly life. What you think is the right thing to do may be your death."

The word *death* rolling out of his mouth made him as dark as the stain covering the heavily wooded apartment. I mean, this guy had a wife, a few kids, and many jobs, and here he was, drinking Scotch with me in the middle of the day in a glorious cave he had created underneath a Harlem apartment building. These were the people I listened to.

The phone rang.

"Yes. Okay. You bring me four large pizzas. We have a lot of people to feed tonight. Yes, that's right. The usual party, right. Please cut them up into small slices. Yes. You know the size. Good. No, I will be out there to pick them up. Not the door. Right."

He hung up the phone and smiled at me, getting up from his sofa, which made a sound of relief.

"Big family to feed?" I asked, trying to change the subject.

"You shouldn't listen to it phone conversations that have nothing to do with you. Besides, what you hear is never what is being said." He started to laugh. "Be light a little. You can do it more good in the light. Now, if you excuse me, I have some bathrooms to get to in the building across the street. Got to keep it all going."

We walked back through the halls from which we came, closing doors and shutting off lights. After we emerged back into the daylight, Armando locked up tight and headed out toward the block, blending in with the motion. I made my way back upstairs.

CHAPTER 5

EMPTY POOLS

1

Neighborhood kids were playing their last game of baseball before the pool at Jackie Robinson Park was filled for the summer. The sound of the ball hitting the bat bounced off the walls of the empty pool and sent waves through the streets. The light aqua blue paint contrasted the brown bricks that surrounded the rest of the momentary universe of the children.

A radio rested on the ridge of the pool and played the latest Hell Rell joint. Buildings that people had walked past quickly not too long ago now had new Brownstone Restoration FOR SALE signs in front. Furniture that didn't fit in the moving vans was stacked on the street. The kids waiting for the next game leaned up against whatever walls weren't under construction.

Headlines in the newspapers left in the stands talked about marches to protest the evictions spreading through Harlem. A picture of Councilman Macon leading the protest made me feel like the neighborhood was being taken care of and that I was in the middle of a place that was fighting for something true.

Sounds of an aluminum bat hitting a ball pinged vibrations. My vision blurred as the children cheered. Suppressed memories opened daydreams dominated by a giant nurse wearing a blue outfit, attempting a soothing tone. A door closed behind her. I could hear Namuna behind the door but couldn't get to her.

Children arguing about whether a ball hit over the SIX FEET DEEP sign was a double or triple snapped me back.

The sight of those kids playing pushed me from the scene in my mind. The further away I got from my job, the nearer my memories became. I ran quickly up Edgecomb Avenue, back to my apartment. Edgecomb was parallel to and in back of St. Nicholas Place, running high above Jackie Robinson Park, which was the end of Sugar Hill. You could see the Bronx from that narrow row of apartments fortunate enough not to be looking into anyone else's windows. Benches held folks taking a break from the sun across from them.

The warm weather brought the barbecues and the smells of home-cooked love covered tight in foil, to be served by age and neighborhood rank. I ran past an old woman sitting in a lawn chair who wouldn't let me go by without letting me know about her.

"The fuck you think you're doing going by me like that?" she said through lips covering gums that had long since lost her teeth.

"I'm on my way home," I said.

"You think I give a fuck about that when you didn't say hello to me or give me the courtesy of noticing that I was there? You say hello every time you see me, hear?"

"I do. I'm sorry."

"That doesn't take away from what you've gone and done. Fucked up my whole afternoon."

I walked away slow, up to the tip of Edgecomb, where it turns and hooks around up to 155th and bends back to St. Nicholas Place. I walked past the entrance to the bridge and watched for a moment as cars tried to navigate the maniacal five-way intersection.

I could hear Bob Sheppard announcing the starting lineups over the PA across the river.

A gypsy cab pulled up and the driver stared at me.

"You need a ride?" he asked.

"No, I live down the block. Thanks anyway."

"Why waste my time then?" he yelled before drinking down a Red Bull. "I have to make a living!" He tossed the can out the window and sped away before it hit the ground.

I walked out to the middle of the street, picked it up, headed back to my building, up the stairs, and into my apartment without being stopped by the characters I was starting to become one of.

There was a note on the fridge.

"First one home gets seltzer! Love ya!"

Knight ran to the front door and started scratching like a madman to get out.

"What? What is it? You want to go next door again?"

He was meowing like crazy. I picked him up and carried him over to Sukal's door and knocked. The locks started to come undone. The door opened quicker this time.

"He was almost asking for you," I said, placing him in her arms. "Does that seem strange?"

"No, not at all," she said, her head leaning on the hand that held the door open. "What have you been working on out there? I heard you last night. It felt good to know that those keys were going again."

"I'm not so sure. Maybe I'm just trying to figure out the world around me," I said. "I think it's moving backwards sometimes."

"The world is moving as it always does. Perhaps you're just seeing what you want to see."

"I lost my job because I couldn't keep my mouth shut."

"Well, that just makes you a believer in yourself. You should find pride in that. So many people today have lost their faith. My Robert never did. Perhaps you are continuing his work of building your own vision, though I can't honestly say if that's a good thing or not."

"I want what I've lost," I said, suddenly and without control.

"Why's that? What's back there for you? Do you think you'd change what you've done? I'm not sure that's so wise to think on. Perhaps you just need to take a good, long look at the past and then move on.

That's how you get over tragedy. That's how I got over mine."

"What is it that I need to look at?"

"I can't tell. Only you know what's getting inside of you. Myself, I have my own past to deal with. Perhaps I'm not quite ready to let go. Maybe you're trying to find something. That's why you're opening up to the world you're writing about. It's risky I know, but in the end, it's all part of life. It'll be worth it.

"Just make sure you spend as much time in reality—that's the here and now—as you do looking back in the past for answers. You won't find anything there. That's how I might have lost my Robert. He wanted to make up time for what he lost working for the city.

"That's exactly what he told me with his last breath. I'm sure that if he could somehow speak to you from wherever he is now, he'd tell you that it's not worth it. Anyhow, I want to spend time with this little man in here for a while. After all, he came to me."

I went back inside our apartment and crawled out onto the fire escape, where I stared across the street at the endless stories taking place behind each window.

2

Transitions between events were fading.

I heard the front door open. Namuna walked in from work carrying two huge bags and a tired set of eyes. She looked a little surprised to see me there, because, for the most part, I was always an A train or two away from her.

"What are you doing home?"

"I got fired today."

"For what?"

"For Christopher Columbus."

"Say that again?"

"I just couldn't pimp out that land that he stole, Boo. Just couldn't. Something inside me snapped."

She stopped for a minute before she answered, taking time to put her bags down and pull out a bottle of water.

"Tell me, who is it exactly you are fighting *for*?" she asked, taking a long sip while looking through me, then walking out toward the fire escape herself, holding her face to the breeze that usually kicks up just before the rain.

"I'm fighting for us."

"Us?" she asked. "You mean you and me?"

"I mean us. All of us. Everyone."

"What makes you believe all of these people want you taking up a fight for them? They have no need for a hero."

"I didn't do what I did because of what people want from me. I did it because of what I want for myself. I want to be the man I should have always been."

"I just want to be sure it's *you*. That's all I need, all I've ever needed."

"You noticed anything strange about things out there today?" I asked, trying to change the subject but realizing that was going to be a little rough.

"What do you mean?"

"Just that everything looks like it slowed down a click or two. People are taking the time to live."

"I haven't seen any of that. I've got two new clients at work and these guys from another firm whose name I can't even pronounce calling me and trying to set up a meeting. I haven't had time to think about anything until now, and I'm taking these moments to think of you."

I looked at the typewriter, then back to her. She stood up and moved away from me, as far as she could. I knew that some of the windows across the street had to be watching the scene between us go down.

"Where's Knight?" she asked. "One of my customers knew I had a cat and brought a little nip for him. Cute pouch, huh?"

"He's next door. Sukal needed a little company."

"Maybe she sees him as her husband come back to her. He's not though. You know that much, right? You're at least that in touch with reality, aren't you?"

I laughed. It's never a good idea to laugh at something your wife says when she's being serious.

"Maybe that's why we moved in next to her, you know?" I told her. "And the typewriter—that was meant for me. Maybe I'll write a little story about that, about a cat that moved in next door, who was really the spirit of a lonely woman's late husband."

She pulled back, grabbed the typewriter, and held it over the fire escape, dangling it over the street below. "I'll smash it to pieces just to wake you up. If you want to do something meaningful, then do it! But don't half-ass your way into thinking little stories about cats and dead husbands are going to change the world. That's not the man I married."

We both paused at the reference to death. I looked at her stomach at the same time she felt for it. The one hand holding the typewriter case was not strong enough, and it dropped quick and crashed hard. I leaned over the rail with her. It hadn't dropped all the way to the street, just to the fire escape below us.

"Well, go on and get it," she said, noticing the look in my eyes. "I'll open a bottle of wine."

I walked quickly down the ladder to the next landing. The case was busted open, but aside from a couple of keys having fallen off, the rest of it looked to be fine. Inside the case, under a piece that had been torn away, I saw a few sheets of blue paper. Blueprints. Before I could look at them, a whizzing sound caught my attention. Inside the window a kid was playing with one of those old racing car games, the ones with a remote control attached to the track and a car that went around and around held into a groove by a metal piece attached to it.

The kid saw me looking in the window, smiled, and went back to playing. I carried the damaged typewriter and its pieces back up to our apartment and climbed in the window. The *I* key was missing and nowhere to be found.

We both walked into the kitchen.

I put the typewriter on the table, and Namuna went to work on it right away, bringing out the old Craftsman toolbox her father had used. She rubbed her hand over the tools as if reaching out over the eyebrows of her father to remember what they felt like. She had lost him not too long ago. There were stories to be told about this great man who'd built their home and everything in it. She used to follow him around as his assistant, wearing his tool belt, which always fell to the floor from her little waist.

She started screwing in what needed to be put back together while I unfolded all the papers on the kitchen table. The papers were full of equations that I could not understand at all, but that Namuna saw and knew at once. The most I had ever been able to do in high school was basic algebra, and even then I would have to write other people's English papers so I could copy off their math tests.

"It's his life's work," I said in awe. "We've found a treasure."

"I would say his treasure is next door with our cat. This is his work, which, now that he's gone, doesn't appear useful to anyone."

"This is his heart," I said, trying to figure out what the blueprints were for.

"Not his heart, just his building designs. Nothing too fancy either, just—well, look at this, that's kind of interesting."

"What? What is it?"

"He spent most of his time creating heating and lighting systems that save on energy and draw from—oh, well, would you look at that!"

"What? What!" I said, surprised to see Namuna so impressed.

"He had the ideas for solar panels on the roof, but look at the date! 1965. Nobody was using solar energy back then. This guy was on to something for sure. I think he wanted the building to be energy-efficient, so . . ."

"Go on," I pleaded. "What are you getting at? I don't see it."

"Well, if you really look, he wasn't actually designing buildings. He was trying to save on the power used by the tenants. I do believe he was trying to bring down their electric bills. Yes, see!"

She turned over one of the blueprints and went over the math equations on the back. "They were not measurements for a building. He was trying to figure out how much each person was paying for electricity. This guy had it too. Wonder what happened. Seems like an awful lot of work never to be seen by anyone."

"Can't we show it now?" I asked, excited. "Is it too late?"

"It's not that it's too late to show anyone, it's that everyone knows about this now. It's nothing new. But back then, if he would have been able to put his plans in the public eye, this gentleman would have made a fortune out of making people's lives easier to live. What a great thing to do with a life—"

She saw me looking away—saw me thinking that this man had done what I wanted to do with my life.

"No," said Namuna, rolling up the blueprints and going back to work on the typewriter until she realized she shouldn't be doing that either.

"What do you mean no? I haven't said anything yet. Don't guess what I'm thinking."

"I don't have to guess. I know you. I just don't want to end up like Sukal, believing that you're coming back to me in the form of a cat. I want you here, with me, now. I have no interest in memories of you."

"It won't be like that for us," I told her. "Besides, I can make my mark on the world and still spend my life with you. Don't you believe that?"

"I want to."

"Then believe it."

A strange silence hung in the kitchen and failed to carry the weight of our conversation out the window. I imagined a camera trucking back and the scene fading away.

CHAPTER 6

THE BOXER

1

I started cleaning on the regular because I had to do something that would keep me from sitting behind a desk. I figured that by meeting everyone on the block I would become part of it, instead of observing and wondering about the best way to package it. My eye was trained that way, and I wanted to unlearn.

There was no desire to write with a purpose anymore. Evolution would come through action. I think every man goes through that in his mid-thirties. At that point in your life you start to believe you have carved out the image of who you are and what you are going to become. There is enough experience on your résumé to allow you to go out and get the same type of gig you've had before. I couldn't become that person. At that point, I was just looking to become another guy on the block, and then something would grow out of that, but I wouldn't force it. The Sweeper they might call me. I didn't care.

With Namuna at work, I didn't want to sit around the house like a bum, so I took my broom out on the block and started to clean. I went down one side, past the Chess-Playing Kids and beneath the people looking out the windows to see if anything was changing in the neighborhood. I stayed clear of the Bodega on the other side of the block because there was always someone standing in front.

I found myself by the Chicken-and-Rice Van, sweeping up in

front of those who were devouring the dishes. The two old folks who were handing out *Watchtower* magazines smiled and tried to give me one, but I said no and kept going.

Some people just assumed I was working for the Chicken-and-Rice Guy, so they started handing me their silver trays instead of just tossing them on the ground. I swept up the pieces of food that fell but stopped when some of the pigeons started attacking the bag.

"Who told you I needed a cleaning man," the Chicken-and-Rice Guy said. "I don't need a cleaning man."

"I'm not cleaning up for you," I told him. "It's for the block."

"You mean you're not going to ask for cash when you're done?"

"Nope," I said. "I'm happy just doing what I'm doing."

"I can give you a plate of food each day you clean, but that's it."

"I'm not asking for that, though."

"But you'll take it," he said, handing me a silver tray with a steaming piece of chicken placed over a bed of rice and salad.

I leaned my broom against the short wall in front of the Bailey House and dug in. I must have passed by that van every day on my way up and down the block but had never stopped to get something to eat. Now, tasting it for the first time, I started to think about what I'd missed. Even though I stained my shirt with the sauce from the chicken, I felt clean inside. I understood why people came from all around to eat this. It was food that took over your body and let your mind relax. Food for the working class that eased instead of poisoned.

A jittery man came up from behind and tossed his Red Bull can to the ground before placing his order. It was the Gypsy Cabdriver who'd nearly run me over last time. He sat down next to me and started devouring his food while talking on his cell phone.

"No . . . I need to go and eat," he said, rice dripping from his mouth and falling onto the concrete. "I'll call you when I'm back on the road. Good."

"Always on the go huh?" I said.

"Should I know you well enough to talk with you because I'm not remembering you at all."

"You yelled at me the other day for taking your time," I told him, placing my tray in the plastic garbage bag and taking the broom back in my hand.

"Then you deserved it, I'm sure," he responded, sucking the meat off the bone and tossing it next to him on the street.

I swept it up and put it in the bag, but he paid no notice. After scooping more into his mouth, he got up, still chewing, left the tray next to him, jumped back into his gypsy cab, and pulled away. The Chicken-and-Rice Guy approached me as I threw away the leftovers from the Gypsy Cabdriver's food.

"See, there is a reason you came to me," he said. "Most of my customers, they are good people. They are respectful of me and my business. However, we cannot help the fact that nothing is a hundred percent. I tell you what. Each day you come by my van to clean, I will give you a meal, how does that sound?"

"I would do it even if you didn't give me anything," I told him. "It's what I want to do."

"Well, perhaps you will come to appreciate favors the more you clean. Let us hope so for both of our sakes."

So it went like that for the next few weeks. I would write in the mornings on the fire escape about the people I met on the block and sweep up during the day. I was well fed and well occupied. There was a normalcy to my routine, which helped me transition from my office life. That routine stopped the day I met the Boxer.

I was sweeping up near the 147th Street station when I saw the Boxer, but it was not the same man I'd known from years past. That guy was really put together. I would see him shadowboxing in the street every day. His shoulders were thick. You could tell he liked the way he looked as well, always wearing a wifebeater with gray sweats, glancing at his own reflection in car windows while he trained.

Kids on their way to school, the little ones at least, would copy his moves, throwing punches in the air as they descended the stairs to the subway.

He was a Golden Gloves hopeful for New York, who worked the late shift at UPS. The road had opened up for him. Had he kept on shadowboxing in the street, had he stayed inside that gym, things would have been Golden Gloves and more for this guy. The unfortunate thing is that even though he shadowboxed all day long, he couldn't take what the shadows threw back.

I noticed him getting thinner and thinner while I was still working at the office. At first, I saw him throwing punches on the street, but he started to call out to the shadows as he swung. The kids started stepping farther away from him and running down the steps to the subway to escape.

Then the jabs got slower and slower and slower. His bobs and weaves became sways. His sweat gave way to dirt. His hair became nappy. In just a few months, what were once strong fists knocking down mountains became open hands asking for coins. Soon after that, a permanent white spittle took up residence in the corners of his mouth.

His road closed. Even if he cleaned himself up, he would never get back into shape enough to claim what was supposed to be his. If it were a movie, he might have opened up a gym for the neighborhood kids to box in, but life isn't like that.

That's why there are movies.

Speaking with random people in New York and trying to piece their stories together into one whole life was dangerous for me. Once I take something in, it's nearly impossible to let it go. However, I needed new information to absorb. It had become habit to me—one I needed to feed.

I swept carefully, but not obviously, toward him and started with a hello. If you do that to most people, even if they are on their way down, they will at least pause for a moment.

I told him my name and he extended his hand. His shake was still powerful. I knew that he could still take someone out—take me out—if he needed to.

"You need something?" he asked, looking at me stone in the eyes as if we were about to go a few rounds and the whole of St. Nicholas Place was going to serve as the ring.

"You used to fight Golden Gloves," I said.

"Want to ask me questions, huh? For what? What the hell you want to know about me for?"

"No disrespect," I told him. "Just that I want to know about the neighborhood. I want to be part of it."

"Nobody wants to be part of this place," he said. "That just happens to them."

"Well, we all have to be part of something," I shrugged. "A block is as good as anything, no?"

He paused for a moment, trying to capture all the thoughts swimming around his brain.

"You think you can help something, someone, just by talking about it?" he said. "Nah, that's not how these stories go."

"What do you think I'm trying to do out here?" I said, showing him the broom and bag of trash. "Talking to people sometimes opens up the ideas for change. That's all I'm saying to you."

"If you want to hear my story, how about you get me something decent to eat. Man feels more relaxed when he's got something proper in his stomach."

"I couldn't agree more," I told him, walking with him up to the Chicken-and-Rice Guy, who handed me my daily dish, which I then turned over to the Boxer.

We sat down on the wall and he started in. Each of his bites was immaculate, and he patted the sides of his mouth with a napkin whenever a little sauce dripped.

"Yeah. I was on the way up," he said after he had fully swallowed one bite. "But on that way, man, you know, you have to eat. You have to survive outside of the ring. That was always the hardest part. You know, those moments when you're just fighting, they just moments, right? A fight don't last but a few minutes anyway if you total up all the time between the bell ringing and all.

"Problems start when folks offer to help. When people from the outside, from outside of your world, start to come in and offer help to you for what looks to be no reason. No agenda."

"I've got nothing to gain by talking to you," I said. "I'm just trying to get clean."

"You and me both, man. You and me both."

He continued eating as if he were dining in the best spot in town. He just might have been. Slowly, the delivery drivers, construction workers, and parking police started to go back to work. All of them came to me to throw their trash away.

"Where do you think things went wrong?" I asked.

"Why you reason something went wrong? I'm right where I need to be. I don't need help getting out of it either. That's what I told you already is how this whole mess started."

"Who tried to help you?" I asked.

"You think I'm that cracked out that you can just flip a story like that on me. That I'm just going to give it up like that. Hey! Hey! This boy right here thinks he got someone *out his mind!* Boy, I ain't halfway out my mind yet. This here condition you see me in is a choice I made."

There was a long pause. The heat of the approaching summer jumped down from the sun. He looked up hard, as if he were trying to blind himself. He exhaled like he was meditating.

"You want to hear it? Goes like this then. I think, well, yeah, back in '02 it was. I had it all on a decent track, right? I mean, I was working for UPS, driving and shit. I was one of those dudes wearing that outfit, making my rounds around downtown. So it was good for me, because those shifts, those shifts were flexible, and I could stay in shape with all those packages, know what I'm sayin'? So things were good for me. I mean, look at me now, all worn down from what I put inside me, but you can still see the frame. You can still see some of what I used to be.

"So there was this one lady that used to work up in this spot down on the East Side. Boy, you know she was fine. Anyways, I would make deliveries to her every day, and we became kind of friendly. We started knowing each other's names, and I could tell that she would be looking at me when I bent down or lifted a package. Those women working hard up in those buildings be needing some man, you know? Harmless at first, right? I mean, I had about ten women like that around town who just like to look at a man, then go home and do themselves proper, right? Well, this woman here, one day, she wanted a little more.

"I went up to her office and asked her to sign for her shit like I normally did, and she gets up and closes the door. Now, I tell you man, she looked good. She had on those boots that day—man, I can still smell that leather. She had on those pull-up stockings that go just above the boots, and her skirt was short, but not ho short, right, so it was just the right amount of leg that showed. Whoa! She sat up on that desk and bent over so I could see them Upper East Side clean tits hanging in that bra. Oh, man. Now I had heard from others not to be messing with any of these women because they were trouble, but you have to understand, man, that I was in training for fights, which meant no women at all. I was bursting. I damn near ripped her skirt off and started rubbing myself all over her panties. The whole office smelled like her juice. Oh, man, it was on!

"Before long I had moved her clothes out of the way and started to go on up inside of her. She started making noises like crazy—you know, she wasn't in control of herself at all, man. Not at all! Anyhow, some old dude from the office comes busting in the door, and after she gets a hold of herself and sees him, well, she starts yelling for help! Oh, man, everyone from the office came in there and starts beating on me.

"One minute I got myself up in this woman and I'm out of it right, not in the mood to fight, and then, before I know what's what, the office is all up on me, pounding my ass. Ain't nobody listening to a word I say. They call up the cops. She fakes tears. I'm in a holding cell. Lose my job. In front of a judge. Get three years. Do them all. Hard time man, *hard* time, you know what I'm saying? Prison ain't no joke. I come out of there, and . . . well, the story that goes from there is pretty much the same as you've probably heard."

His eyes were red, and if they had the ability to tear up, they would have. After he handed me his empty tray of food, he walked away, shaking pennies in his hand.

I swept furiously around where he had been standing, but no matter what I did, new pieces of trash kept rolling over the spot I was trying to keep clean.

2

"I got an offer," Namuna said, before I could even put my cleaning supplies away. "It's going to be perfect for both of us, but at the start, it might be a little rough. Let's open a bottle before we start talking about it."

She poured me a glass and asked that I sit down for a minute. Though I was trying to concentrate on her, the story that the Boxer had just told me was playing over and over in my head. I'm not sure I could have survived something like that. Worse than that, I had been in an office similar to the one he was talking about.

"I got an offer to design a place in Dubai. It's a school. Unlimited budget."

"That's far away," I said, not realizing until after the words had left my mouth that my first reaction had been about me, instead of congratulating her.

"Think of the opportunity, though. And the money is unreal. They're giving me a hundred grand, plus paying for everything over there. You don't have to wander the streets like a maniac with a broom anymore."

"That's not what I'm doing out there," I said, trying to keep the dirt on my hands hidden.

"You'll have to explain it to me one day, because I don't get it," she said, drinking a good portion of her glass. "Why don't you try and write something noteworthy and get the recognition you deserve? That's where your talent is. Don't waste it."

"I might write about all of this when I'm done," I said. "But for now . . . now I have a chance to accomplish something. I can make a difference and leave my mark. It's time for me to do that."

"Once you're gone from this earth, your mark means nothing."

"That's not true," I said, taking a sip of my wine. "I don't think it is. Anyway, let's not go on about this. Tell me about the offer."

"That's right," she said. "I almost forgot completely. See, that's how much I love you. That's how much a part of my life, my thoughts, you are. Us is the important thing, it's the foundation we're going to build our lives on. But for now, this chance I'm getting is going to clear the way. It's our chance."

"I wanted to be the one to give us that chance," I said.

"You were supposed to tell me how proud of me you were," Namuna replied softly. "We'll never get that moment back again. You're lucky I'm not all that sentimental."

"How long would you be gone for?" I asked.

"Six months at least. Probably more like a year though. Should I not take it?"

"I can't tell you that. It's your dream. You should . . . it's just that . . . I don't know. We're so close now. I couldn't imagine not waking up next to you."

"After this gig, we'll be living well."

"We're living well now."

"It could be better."

"It could be worse," I said, smiling, slightly drunk and very much in love with my wife's confidence in herself. "An unlimited budget, huh?"

"Un-fucking-limited!" she said jumping on top of me. "These guys have so much money it's unreal!"

"Is it safe for women over there?" I asked, perhaps looking for the last reason that she shouldn't go, even though I knew inside that she had to.

"Safe? That city is the future of the world."

She saw me drifting deep into my own head and tried to pull me out of it.

I stepped on the fire escape with Namuna and the bottle of wine. We watched the sun go down over the block while the kids played in the fire hydrants and the older ones sat on the stoop talking about what to do that night. We took the time to watch it all go down.

CHAPTER 7

THE A TRAIN

1

After riding the A train to JFK with Namuna and then taking the local all the way back, there was still no rush for me to get home from the 155th Street station. So I grabbed a broom I had stowed where Armando kept the trash and tried my best to make a meditation out of the repetitive motion of my sweeping.

The Preacher smiled at my actions while closing down his storefront church. He had soft skin that was puffed out on his face.

His voice was nearly gone from his sermon, and now instead of shouting feverishly into the microphone, he spoke quietly and pronounced each syllable.

"I have seen you around, doing cleanings in the neighborhood," he said, his voice straining to make eloquent sounds. "My attempts at telling people in my church to pick up after themselves have not produced results."

"I don't mind cleaning up after them," I told him. "I'm helping get something done. That gives me pleasure, you know?"

"I do," he replied. "I achieve such a feeling when I hold the microphone. It is why I yell, which, I'm sure, you've heard spill out to the streets from time to time."

He locked up the gate and looked toward where I had just come from, as if he was looking for somebody. He sighed when nobody appeared.

"Are you hungry?" he asked, still looking over my shoulder. "I always have such an appetite after one of my sermons, and it is seldom—but not as seldom as it should be—that I indulge in the magnificence of the Chicken and Pizza place. If you don't have any plans, I could use some company."

We headed into the spot where Chicken Bob stood as the late-night host, properly attired in his black-and-white tuxedo fur. I thought Knight was lucky as hell not to be hanging out in doorways waiting for scraps to fall. Inside, the lights were bright fluorescent. The man working behind the thick bulletproof glass knew the Preacher well and called out his order when he walked in the door. I ordered myself a four-piece wing combo and waited with him.

Neighborhood folks with their heads dipped low waited as well. People just getting off work looked happy that they'd be eating the magnificent flavors they smelled in no time.

"Not too long ago, I would come in here with my wife and have late-night meals," he said to me, still glancing toward the street between looks at me. "These days, I just have to go looking for her. It wasn't always like that though."

"I don't understand," I told him, just now realizing that he was in need of conversation with someone and have them listen for real to what he was saying.

"She has been taking this medication that helps her deal with pain, but I'm afraid it has taken away some of her mind as well. Usually if she's not home around this time, I have to go looking for her."

"How do you know where to find her?" I asked.

"It's not hard, she's always at the same place. The A train. I know all the station conductors by now, so I just call them to find what car she's on. At first it was very frightening, but now it has become habit."

He used whatever strength he had in his lungs to manage a laugh that quickly turned into a cough. He washed it away with his cherry soda.

"That's not going to make you any better," I said.

"I'm good. I'm good. Just that keeping track of that woman is difficult after my sermons. I try to make sure she only takes a few spoonfuls of that medicine at home, but when she goes and takes the whole bottle, well, we get into trouble then."

They called our order and I got up to retrieve the chicken through the little bulletproof revolving door on the counter.

"Doing things like eating fried chicken at late-night spots should be done—and is best done—with somebody you love," he said, slowly opening up his chicken box like a child hoping to find the gift he had been asking for all year.

He passed a picture of his wife across the table, took a bite, and leaned back with the food in his mouth.

"Here, this is her," he said after swallowing. "Well, she looks a little different these days, but the eyes are the same. The eyes always stay the same."

"She's beautiful," I told him.

"I know. I am very tired tonight, and if I had not seen you here, I would have jumped on the train myself. But since you are here, since you are young, since you seem like you are a person looking to help, I was wondering if you wouldn't do me a favor and bring her home tonight. I feel like I haven't the strength to do it."

"What makes you think that I would go looking for your wife at this time of night?" I said, a little startled that he would ask such a personal favor. Back then, before I was really inside, I didn't understand how the neighborhood worked. How everybody here raised each other because mothers were working and fathers were working harder, or just gone. You took on that responsibility if you were part of the block. For them, it was not a want or desire to be part of something, it just was how life was lived. So, if you were walking down the street and someone asked you to get something for them at the store, you went and did it. If you didn't, there was no punishment, but you were just not treated as part of the block, and without that, you were just a resident.

"I think you are someone who is looking to be part of something," he said. "To do that, you need to do favors and walk down paths you are not used to walking. You never know when you'll need me for something. You have been given things that you needed but did not ask for, yes?"

"How did you know that?" I said.

"Because Sukal is one of my oldest friends and has been attending my church for years. Her husband would never come down from his fire escape long enough to listen to the word of God. He did not believe too much in any of that. And you, well, I see you up there using his typewriter. You are trying to do what?"

"I'm just trying to empty out my head," I told him, realizing it for myself in the same moment. "It doesn't seem like that simple of a task though."

"Nothing is simple like that. You are putting sounds out into the night, are you not? You are sending echoes through these old blocks, are you not? Perhaps I heard your shouts and am answering you with a question that happens to be in the form of a favor. It was you who called out to me from above."

"You were asking God to answer you, though," I said. "Maybe I was just blocking his message to you."

"And perhaps—perhaps he sent it through you."

"Do you really think God has any intention of answering you?" I asked.

"I do. I have to believe that."

"Why?"

"Because, my friend, if I did not believe in that, then what has my life been all about? What have I spent so much time preparing these sermons for and getting these people to believe in what I tell them? No. No. It couldn't have been a lie. It just couldn't have been."

With that, he grabbed his box of chicken, flipped up his collar, and headed home.

2

During the busy parts of the days, the crowd in the subways is so malt thick there is no space for identity. You are part of the rush of blood that has to feed the city, and if you're lucky, when it's your turn to get out the doors, you have enough of your own mind left to enjoy your walk home and think back over how lucky you were to have contributed that day to the city.

However, in the deepest parts of night, the parts that bleed into the ridiculous portions of the morning, there *is* enough room to think.

Between the subway cars in New York, there are steel doors you can open and close to move from one car to the next. There is a moment when you're riding outside the cars but inside the tunnels. If you can stand the smell, it's an amazing trip, though dangerous, because you have no idea what's hanging from the ceilings of the tunnels, or if the train is going to stop suddenly or not.

A youngster selling M&M's and Starburst out of taped-together candy boxes moved freely between the cars. It wasn't until he was gone that I realized it was the Kid who had been sitting on the bridge waiting for the sun to come up over Yankee Stadium.

On the last car, I saw a woman eating a box of Dots and struggling to pick up a pack of Newports that had just fallen to the ground. In the pocket of her jacket, I saw a medicine bottle, like a bottle of cough syrup, open and exposed to the subway air.

She looked up and saw me recognize her.

"Oh, here be the 'come and get her' police again. I'm not ready to stop riding. Either that or I can't figure out just how I'm going to get off this here train."

"Your husband sent me," I said. "I'm just trying to bring you home."

"Well, we are most definitely heading downtown and beyond right now, so you're going to have to wait until we get out to JFK if you want to take me all the way back uptown. That's a long ride, but I have tons of stories to make it better."

"I was just out there today," I said, sitting myself down across from her. "Not really in the mood to go back so soon. Why not just do me a favor and let me take you home? Your husband is worried."

"I don't know you well enough to do you a favor," she said, raising her voice. None of the people around us noticed, as they were all inside of their own late-night stories. "Did he have my kids with him?" she asked, taking a swig of her medicine. "We have four you know. Four, now. He has so many more what with his church, though. That's good for him.

"We used to go out to the beach. It was the D train out to Coney Island. Coney is the last stop on the line. Usually on Memorial Day or the Sunday before Memorial Day we'd go. Oh, we had a great time all of those summers. I told each of them that they'd get two dogs from Nathan's."

She lost herself and popped a few more Dots into her mouth, but having her mouth full didn't stop her from speaking.

"That last time we went out there, it was the final stop on the D train, just like we are going to the last stop on the A train. I already told you that, though. You can catch either train from 145th. Well, on the way, like I always did, I told them to be careful, because the closer to the shore they were, the closer to Mom they were. 'Nothing can hurt you if you stay close to Mom,' I told them.

"My youngest, he would just do things like he wanted. Some people can't help that. So my boy went out to the shore of the ocean. He just loved to look out over things. He was a big-picture thinker. Patient, like he was studying everything he looked at like a map.

"Well, he wanted to see more and more, so he just moved inch by inch farther away from the shore. I couldn't even tell that he was moving away from me. Oh, I told him not to go out too far. I had three other kids to look after and he knew that, but he never thought he needed any looking after.

"I looked back to the direction where he was supposed to be and I saw this big old Russian man running into the water, and when he walked back to the beach, there was my boy, just still as could be in his arms.

"Still as could be," she repeated, more mouthing the words than saying them.

"I wish I could tell you something other than I'm sorry," I said, barely able to get the words out.

"You know, that was the last stop on the D line," she said, in no response to me. "I take the A train now because it starts at the same place but ends somewhere different. I guess I'm just hoping for a different ending. That doesn't make me crazy, does it?"

"No crazier than anyone else," I told her. "I'll sit with you until the last stop. Then we'll go home."

We rode in silence all the way to Far Rockaway and back on the A for the next hour and a half. By the time I got her in front of her building, the only light on was the Preacher's on the second floor.

"Mr. Hernandez! Mr. Hernandez!" I yelled up. "I've brought her home to you."

He came to the fire escape and smiled down at us. We both knew that she would try again another day for a different ending to her story, but that night, she was home.

Safe.

The nighttime had not lifted yet. No cats along the street. Even the gas station that was always open for business was calm, with not a single gypsy cab pulling up for service. It was a rare moment in the city, when nobody wanted anything.

The Bodega was silent as well.

It started to rain one of those hot New York summer rains that did nothing to cool the moment. Quick heels walking down 155th echoed the drops. I looked up and saw a face that seemed familiar, but I couldn't place it. She noticed me right away.

"You look different not all bent over on your fire escape pounding away on those keys," she said, then paused for a moment to give me a chance to recognize her. "You got it now?"

Her eyes were huge, the lipstick she used was tasteful, and her cheeks were nearly flawless, without a hint of makeup. I was blushing hot under the falling rain at the shape of her body and its proximity to mine.

"You live across the street from me," I said as the rain let up just a bit.

"I thought you might play it where you pretended not to know who I was," she said, leaning up against the lamppost.

"I don't play things like that. I don't need to anymore," I said back, waving my ring finger.

"How long is she gone for?" she asked.

"How much are you watching me?"

"A woman usually watches a man more than he knows. You are not all that discreet about things. Got a light?"

"Don't smoke. I never believed in black-and-white movies."

That one got her.

"Can you walk a girl home? It's late."

I couldn't resist the temptation to dance just a little bit. After all, there was no chance of getting caught, and I wasn't doing anything wrong. I knew exactly where she lived.

We stood at her stoop, under the same window we'd watched each other through.

"You coming up?" she asked.

"I'm going home. This here is as far as we're going to go. Understand me?"

"I feel your words but can't get your actions. I don't offer this to just anyone, you know. There are boys calling at all hours for just a chance. For just a taste of what I'm leaving open for you."

"Perhaps you should let them have that chance. That way when they reach my age and become who I am, they are not as conflicted as I feel right now."

"It's that conflict that makes me want—"

She stopped short, leaving the last words hanging in the heavy air. I turned to leave.

"You need to go upstairs now," I said.

"I'm not taking my offer away," she said, walking the stairs, knowing she was being watched. She took forever to slink up the few steps of her stoop and in through the vestibule door.

From down St. Nicholas Place, I could see a figure approaching rapidly, like a gray rhino charging through the dark night, taking each block with a ferocious quickness. My heart pounded. Anyone who was around would see everything but say nothing. I held fast, knowing that I didn't have the speed to flee. The rhino got closer, and soon I saw that it was a man in a gray sweatsuit with the hood pulled over his head.

The sounds of grunting and breathing took over the air. He reached me but paid no mind, continuing up the block, until he hit 155th, at which point he spun around and charged back toward me. As he came, I was sure that this time I would not be left standing. Normally, there is a slight rumble from the subway below, but the force from this movement was being exerted by something from above the concrete.

As he ran past this time, I could fully make out the face of the man underneath the hood. It was younger, filled with muscle and hope. The Boxer. It was him. How? He continued down the block, then back up again.

The sun rose.

I looked up to the top of St. Nicholas Place and saw the Kid walking down 155th with a taped box of M&M's under his arm, heading toward the bridge.

"Thanks for helping out my mom," he said.

"She said you drowned," I replied. "Is it true?"

"I guess it is. I don't really think about what happened in the past."

"But that means you're dead. How can you be sitting here talking to me if you're dead? Doesn't that mean I'm dead too?"

"No. It just means that when we die, we don't leave. We just remain, for the most part, unseen. For you, I guess you passed by that graveyard one too many times. We're just there because the folks who are alive don't want to let go. They can't accept the fact that we're gone. It's their devotion to living in the past that keeps us around. We exist only for those who need us."

"Are you saying I need you?"

"I'm saying that you haven't let go of your past yet. When you do that, you'll be able to start helping those around you."

He was gone before I could ask anything else.

A few crows from the graveyard flew over his head as he walked away. By me, the pigeons picked at the tossed-out pizza crusts on the ground. Chicken Bob and the Bodega Cat both made their way past me and took their respective places. The Boxer ran up and down the block ten more times.

I headed up to my fire escape as the block rattled underneath from the vibrations of the moving A train.

CHAPTER 8

LETTING GO

1

I hadn't used my laptop since Sukal gave me the typewriter. No Internet, emails, blogs. The typewriter was my only tool. The more I left the laptop unused, the less I felt the need for it. It was strange—it started to take on a different look. It looked, well, new. The story of the laptop was nowhere near as romantic as the typewriter. I remembered when I first got it.

I left the moment and lost myself in another flashback.

It wasn't early in our relationship, but we weren't ready for the responsibility of a child. I was of the mind, as was Namuna, that we needed time to be in love and travel around before we started a family. I'd already seen what having a child too early can do to a marriage.

So there I was, pacing around in the garden. It was there not only to provide a sense of calm but also to prevent outsiders who didn't know what went on in the building from seeing in. I can't tell you how many times I must have driven by and not known what was behind those trees. I'm not even sure I noticed the trees.

I had to go outside to steal an Internet connection so that I could IM on the new laptop my company had given me. I kept leaving the waiting room to find reception, a connection. The last time I'd come back to the waiting room, Namuna had gone in. The meeting had been canceled, and I'd been hanging on the IM all by myself when she'd been called in. The time moved slow as I waited, holding onto that damn laptop without any reception.

I asked the nurse at the desk what was happening, and she told me to sit down. She was nice and tried to be calming, but she had seen hundreds of men like me before. We all had that same look on our face, like we weren't doing the right thing. It's not that going through with it was the wrong choice, but it was the realization that *I* was not really going through anything—it was Namuna that was going to be left with the physical memories forever.

The company I was working for was happy with me and leaning toward hiring me on full-time. With the money they were offering, I could have afforded a family right then. Maybe I should have rushed in and stopped it, but I did not have it in me to make a decision. I was, and still am, haunted by that moment each time I see a child.

The door finally opened, and the nurse told me I could go in and see her. She was wrapped in a blanket and just waking up from the drugs. She turned over to look at me, with a tear rolling down her cheek.

We walked slowly in the heat back to the car. I remember hating the sun for beating down on us. I guess New York appealed to me because those giant buildings helped to block that out. Her sunglasses covered more than her eyes. I held in everything.

After we got home and I laid her on the couch, I looked out over those palm trees and open sky. I knew then that I would have to leave it all behind.

2

I walked up Edgecomb to this little café that had just opened up on the block. Not sure what it had been before. There were trees surrounding it that blocked out the projects below. The Bronx was in the distance. Next to me was a suited woman talking into her Bluetooth in that way that made her look like she was talking to herself. She noticed me and didn't take the time to smile until she needed a light for her smoke. It was Brenda Hamilton, the real estate agent.

"Quit a few years ago," I told her.

"Perhaps that's a sign I should do the same," she said.

"Well, you have to take those when they come."

"That's a pretty forward comment to give to someone you just met," she replied.

"We know each other," I replied. "You once tried to serve me strawberry jam."

Brenda Hamilton was one of those women who moved with no hesitation. Even as she was talking to me, she kept glancing down and sending out texts.

"What a great campaign that was, if I do say so myself. That place went right away," she said. "If you're still interested in buying, I have a few more that recently opened up but won't stay available for too long."

"I'm happy where I'm at," I told her.

She finished the rest of her pastry.

"What are you doing out here in the middle of the day?" she asked.

"I guess you can say I am between jobs."

"What do you do?"

"I don't do what I did anymore."

"I see. Are you enjoying talking in code, or would you like to speak as if you were an adult?"

"I was a copywriter."

"A writer?" she said, holding up one of the books on the table in front of her.

"A copywriter."

"Well, we're always looking for people with the ability to clarify an idea," she said, looking at me, attempting to figure out what was inside. "Why don't you send me over your portfolio and we can see if you're a fit?"

"I left a job that clarified ideas," I said before her phone went off and she started talking again, holding her forefinger up to make sure I didn't interrupt.

"Well, you just go and tell him that we are not interested in his inability to make a payment, only the payment. In fact, don't tell him that. I'm sure that our lawyer can take care of conveying that message to him. Yes. Yes. Just call the lawyer and that should set things in motion. Yes. What? I need you to call Michelle's school and make sure we gave them enough this year to ensure her status until she . . . yes, that's right. You know how to deal with it. Okay. Thank you so much. See you later before the meeting. Please have my notes . . . right. Good. Bye."

"Kids?" she asked as soon as she finished talking.

"No."

"They change your priorities. Where were we at? You wanted to send me your portfolio, right?"

"I'm trying to create something from my own vision, not add to anyone else's," I said, annoyed that she wasn't paying attention to me. "That's what I'm about these days."

"So that's why you're out of work," she said, without much of a change in expression on her face. "Let me tell you something. We are all—all—a part of someone's vision, it's just that you have to be an expert in what you want to control. Being that you're out here in the daytime, looks like you're just controlling yourself."

"That's enough for me," I told her.

She typed something on her BlackBerry and as she did, I noticed the Kid at the bottom of the block. I motioned to him.

He waved me off, disappearing from sight with his bucket hat covering a good part of his earlobes.

"So if you're not working and not looking for work, what may I ask is it that you're doing?" she said, shielding her eyes from the sun that had just started to fully shine.

"I'm cleaning up my block."

"Well see, that at least sounds interesting," she said, finally smiling. "You need to use that as an introduction next time you meet someone."

She downed the rest of her coffee and only took half a second to brace herself against its heat.

"Look, you have my card. Give me a call if you come to your senses. I'm from around here, so I don't mind helping out people from the neighborhood."

"Sounds like you're helping sell out the neighborhood," I said.

"What was that?" she said, calming herself before she boiled. "I remember being called 'school bitch,' walking home with my books from up the block. Now I'm *running* the block while those fools who called out to me are still on the same piece of it, trying to find someone to blame for their situation. You shouldn't talk about what you don't know."

"You're still here as well," I said.

"This is true, but I'm part of shaping the definition. They are being defined. I'm not sure what you're doing, but I like the way you put your words together quickly."

She laid down another card on the table, left enough money for both our coffees, and straightened her Yves St. Laurent suit with the same motion she used to stand up.

"You can keep these if you like," she said of the books stacked on the table. "I picked up a bunch of the street lit from the stands on 125th. I don't read much of it, just look at the covers, see how they do it, then propose similar things to some publishing execs in midtown. I do some side work as a youth target consultant. It's not my main source of income, but I have the bandwith to do more than one job. Well, give me a call if you want to come back to reality. If not, I'm sure I'll see you again. We're not stopping."

I knew they wouldn't.

CHAPTER 9

HORSES

1

Inside Central Park there are people dying, men dropping down on one knee to propose, young couples enjoying the simplicity of a passionate kiss, old couples trying to find new paths to walk, single women glancing over the tops of the books they're reading to see if anyone is worth escaping fiction for, joggers trying to tone their bodies enough to look good in a suit come Monday, and, of course, there was me—a man walking around, thinking that if I could just clean up a little piece of nature, I might feel worthy to think of myself as a conqueror, like the statues found around every turn in the park.

I found myself leaning on the wall on the north side of 59th Street, just outside the park where the smell of horseshit didn't distract the tourists from taking pictures of the iconic beasts. Large families from the Midwest, weighed down by chicken-fried steak and expectations of the big city, hop in those horse-and-buggy rides for romantic journeys around the park. Do they ever think about the horse? Do they look down and see the nails drilled through their hooves, enabling them, the tourists, to ride through paved streets that were once great trails?

The horses were standing in a line, waiting to pull weight around the park. A man was attempting a clean picture of his wife and son sitting in the carriage.

"Want to get a picture of all three of you?" I asked.

After looking the husband in the eye to convince him that I

wasn't interested in stealing his camera, I had framed them and was about to shoot when the horse looked me deep in the eyes and pissed on himself.

Snap. That was going to make a perfect picture for his office desk.

I decided to believe the look I got from the horse with the black marble eyes. He was telling me about the pain he was in. Going on about how exhausted he was from dragging people around the park. About how cold he was at night. "Let me go. Let me go," he seemed to be screaming. Those were the words I put to what he was trying to convey. Creativity can be detrimental.

"Don't get too caught up in feeling bad for those beasts," a voice called out to me. "They deserve each mile they walk. They do. They do."

The voice belonged to an old lady wearing an outdated Brooks Brothers suit and holding a clear plastic bag of nuts in one hand, a large bottle of water in the other, and several empty plastic butter containers under her arm. She looked up into one of the trees.

"You'll have to come down now, Warren," she pleaded skyward. "I really don't have all day this time."

She filled one of the butter containers with water, placed it on the ground, and dipped into the bag of nuts, tossing them below the trees. The squirrels came running down.

"How do you know what I'm thinking about those horses there?" I asked. "I wasn't talking out loud."

"Well, dear, any decent human being would be thinking along the same lines, but just as I stated, they deserve what they get. They do. I know that. My name's Rena Goldsmith, and these are my trees and my squirrels. You can ask anyone. They've written stories about me, you know."

She checked her watch and moved to another tree.

"Come on Harry. Vanessa. Mags. I've plenty of places to be," she said, becoming a bit more liberal with her nut dispersal, seeing as how she was getting closer to the bottom of her bag. "You know, some of these little fellows are very spoiled from the quality of nuts I give them. Mostly they dine on cashews and pecans, so if anyone else just tries to give them peanuts, they're likely to refuse."

"What did these horses do to deserve being treated like slaves?" I asked.

She walked up to the last tree on her feeding route.

"Most are the drivers who used to whip them and ride them around until they dropped. Yes, sir, when they came back around again for this go of life, they were made the horse. Nothing goes unpunished. Some of them were bad in other ways. Here, let me show you just what I mean. The one you were looking at? Well, dear, I always keep my eye on him."

We walked along the edge of the park until we came to the exit where you could either walk into the city or onto one of the yellow line subways. Out on the street, a white horse with an off-color coat and eyes that no longer bothered to look beyond the blinders hunched over and waited for the day to end.

"That ugly fellow over there! Yes, I'm speaking directly to you there." The horse picked up its head at the sound of her voice. "That ugly beast over there was the worst thing of all. That . . . that *thing* . . . you see the piece on him."

She was talking about his huge dick.

"When he was a man, he was ruled by his penis. You all are. Some can control it better than others. He had a bad habit about airline attendants. He loved those little girls all dressed up in their uniforms. Would take the A train out to JFK and then a bus to the terminal just to wait for them in a car he'd rent. He had some wild times in those days. Plenty of little outfits lay at the feet of beds while young girls filled themselves with marijuana and martinis and let go on top of him. He had a big piece even when he was human. Liked to keep the hats on as well.

"But the problem with that is, he had a wife waiting at home for him, sometimes falling asleep and sometimes working an extra shift or taking a class trying to make herself better. But it wasn't ever quite good enough for him. Never."

"What is it you want now?" I asked.

"It's what I don't want. I don't wish to be here looking like a crazy woman feeding squirrels and talking to horses. I want to take slow walks through the park with my husband and get into little fights over the directions we take. This is not the end of the life I want. Can you do something about that? If you could, if you *would*, I'd be grateful for longer than you could imagine."

With that, she went on her way, disappearing into the park. The old horse looked straight ahead.

I turned around and walked until I found myself under a giant statue of Christopher Columbus on Broadway and 59th Street. Columbus Circle. Getting away from whom I'd become was going to be more difficult than I thought. I started to understand why the people in my neighborhood never left the block.

2

I guess I'd always looked like someone who would listen to other people's stories. I never turned away from them on the train. I am sure now that it was a combination of my need to listen and their need to tell that created the attraction. Those stories are buried inside them, deep down inside, like a spirit trapped.

I had walked up from 59th Street hoping to avoid talking to anyone and found myself where 155th dead-ends against the Hudson River.

I never stood a chance.

"My daddy loved the horses," she said, sitting on the bench watching the garbage barge sail down the Hudson. "He loved everything about them."

She trailed off, whistling a tune that made me recognize her from the No. 1 train.

"You mean he had them in stables?" I asked, even though I should have just kept going.

"No. We never had the money for anything like that. He kept promising me if he made it big, if one of his long shots came across the wire in time, well, he'd buy me one. He was a country boy, you know."

"I didn't know that," I told her. For some reason, they always thought I knew the background to their stories. I never did.

"Well, he did hit on a few long shots right, but they always came during the first race. By the time he left the track, he never had anything left. He'd bring me the racing forms, though. I loved to look at those with him. The names were always fun to read."

She watched the barge move farther down the Hudson, inch by inch.

"Where do you think all the trash goes? I've wondered that since I was little."

She dangled her feet off the end of the bench, kicking them back and forth in the wind, then continued to reflect, as if she were moving back in time, her memories moving along slow with the barge.

"He had a newsstand downtown by one of those old churches. There are so many of them in the city. Oh, I would love to go down there. I thought he was the most powerful man in the world because everyone gave him money and took this newspaper and that magazine. I got them all. He would get up really early and leave. We lived way out in Queens back then. My mother was a cosmopolitan kind of girl and she wanted to live the full life New York City promised and buy a place closer to the newsstand. I told you already he was a country boy. He wanted to stay that way, so we got a place in Long Island after a while. There were horses up there, too, but we never had one.

"Oh, I would go by some of the stables and look, but my mom would always drag me along quick because she wanted no part of living out there. Anyways, that newspaper stand. So many men in great suits would come by there. My daddy always loved to talk with them. He made good money. He took care of us, but it wasn't enough for my mother.

"He never wanted to live in the city. His father owned a sporting goods store upstate. It was a good family business that did well and survived everything, even the Depression. One day, my dad just had a feeling something was wrong. He rushed back upstate and found that his father had a heart attack. He was a young man. A young man with tons of debt. Worse than that, he had another son, who wasn't half the man my dad was. He used to run guns to Canada. I guess that sounds exciting when you talk about it like it's a movie; but when it's life, it's not that exciting at all. No, my father took over the shop. He paid his father's debts, and my mother, though she didn't want to do it, moved upstate.

"Then my uncle took a big order of guns up to Canada. Said he had a hot buyer. This was Depression time. My dad was young, around twenty-two or something. He didn't have the passion for business. He wanted to live outside, away from machines, but he was an honorable man, so he kept the store going. My uncle had other ideas. The gun order was the biggest so far, and my father borrowed heavily against the store."

The barge had made its way far downriver by that point.

"He never came back from Canada. Never. My father lost the store. My mother, she came from a good family, lots of servants and money. She was used to that city life. But that was the Depression— you probably don't know too much about those times. Anyhow, at that time they—'they' being her family—lost everything, except for that one newspaper stand. That was the stand that my father worked every day until the day he died of a heart attack. I hated that day. It was raining. Hard. I hate the rain.

"When he died, it was just my mom, my sister, and I, and my sister was already married and pregnant. You couldn't get rid of kids like you do today. I went with my sister to get the abortion, but that place was just a dirty apartment in some bad scene. I don't remember much other than the darkness. She couldn't go through with it. I don't blame her much for that. I couldn't have done it either.

"But my mother and I were left alone. At that point, I'm pretty sure she hadn't ever written a check. She didn't know how.

"When she was cleaning out the closet of my father's things, she found shoe boxes full of receipts with numbers she didn't understand. Soon she would. I would too. I guess my father had been holding numbers and washing money for various rackets in the city. That kind of stuff was happening all the time. He was holding money too. He had a system of skimming but got caught when he died because the system he came up with died with him.

"My mother brought me to the man we owed money and told him we were all alone and couldn't pay. The only money we had was what the state was giving us because of my father's death. She used me to gain sympathy. She took the money the government gave her for me and paid our debts. That was *my* money. My dead daddy money. Some guy threatened to throw acid in my face if we didn't pay up. That was where my checks went. I worked from then on. I was always trying to make up for what was taken from me, I guess.

"It's a nice breeze today, isn't it? I think it is. I still go down to Central Park to look at the horses go around. It reminds me of those times when I lived out in that nice house with my family. I'm alone in the city now. That's the way my mother wanted it. Not me.

"Would you like to take a walk with me? I'm a little tired from digging so deep into my memory."

"Sure," I told her. "I don't live that far from here."

"I've seen you around. You live over on St. Nicholas Place, don't you?"

"I do."

"Fourth floor. You're always up there on that fire escape working the typewriter. Oh, I like the sounds of that. Not the typewriter mind you, but a man at work. Nothing better than that. You see so many young men these days just sitting there on the steps. It's a shame. What is it that you're working on?"

"I'm not so sure anymore," I told her. "But I don't mind that."

"Maybe we're all extensions of each other," she said, putting her hand on my elbow. "Well, it's nice to think like that anyways."

I looked up and saw that we were in front of the cemetery.

She walked away slowly, not giving me any type of goodbye. Not reaching for my hand to create a moment. She walked over the bridge to the Bronx and faded into the New York traffic.

3

Namuna was waiting in front of our apartment building with one bag hanging over her shoulder and a tan face that exploded into a smile when she realized the figure walking toward her was me.

I forgot everything I had done to occupy myself while she was gone. We kissed in lasting moments under the newly repaired lamppost outside.

"I missed you," she said deeply inhaling my smell and then moving her nose out toward the street. "And I missed this block. This city."

My next memories were of us moving together in bed.

Her tongue felt like the first girl I ever kissed for real when I was thirteen, and that taste was the only known passion in the world. She brought it back again. Making love after was only an extension of that kiss. We dove in and splashed all over each other until there was not a drop left.

When you finish making love on a hot city night, there is nothing more to accomplish. The trains were moving below us. It's not so much that you can hear them going, but you know they're moving under you. There's always direction being taken and choices being made.

Outside our drawn curtains, women in other bedrooms paced around looking for someone to look at them. Lonely men leaned out of their windows and smoked cigarettes, while married ones took a look at the street to see if there was any excitement going on. Up 155th the graveyard stirred. Across the bridge, games were being played, but up here, in this fourth-floor walk-up apartment, for the moment, we were still. We were still.

CHAPTER 10

SPONSORSHIP

1

Since I had lost my job, the block had been my solace outside of Namuna, so I was doing everything in my power to keep it clean. One man can actually do quite a bit on a long stretch of concrete. With each pass I made up and down the block, the people around me started to become more comfortable with what I was doing and began to accept me.

To keep from stockpiling in my brain all the stories they were telling me, I woke up each morning and pounded them out on the typewriter so I would not carry them with me into the night. There were no saved editions and nothing to be distributed to anyone. Everything I produced was to get the mess out of my head and give me space to think, to concentrate on my job.

Some of the folks, who in the past might have let their dogs shit on the sidewalk instead of picking up after the beasts, thought twice because they had seen me—the person sweeping up. They had made a human connection to someone actually doing good, and when that happens, any act of defiance, like dumping a bag of chips into your mouth and tossing the bag on the sidewalk, is not as easy to do.

The Chess Kids continued their games, but as they did, I noticed the area around them was getting cleaner. At one point, when a youngin from their apartment building tried to toss his cherry Coke onto the street, he got a little bit of a beat-down. They nodded at me as I walked by sweeping, allowing me to do my job.

In my head, I had the rest of my life planned out on the block. Namuna would become an in-demand architect and I would do my part on the street, writing for pleasure—or rather, necessity—in the mornings before going on about my task.

The Boxer, for whom I had arranged a daily plate of chicken and rice—my chicken-and-rice payment—was now getting back in shape. Perhaps some of the nourishment was fighting the crack.

"You doing the block some good," the older of the Chess Kids said to me. "I never realized what a cool block we had been living on, so just wanted to give you that respect." He went on with his game, never looking me in the eye.

Taking away some beer bottles from in front of the Foodtown, I noticed someone watching me. Damned if it wasn't a young kid wearing a fedora and holding one of those moleskin notebooks close to his chest. Around his neck hung an old Canon AE1 camera.

When I looked over at him, he tried to play it off like he was taking pictures of the surrounding buildings.

"Can I help you with something?" I called out.

"You're the Harlem Sweep-Up Guy, right?" he said, putting the pen behind his ear and walking the walk of someone much older than he was. "I'm just a reporter looking for a story."

"What paper are you with?"

"I'm what you might call an independent journalist," he said, smiling big. "I'm looking to catch on with someone, and I think your story can help me do that. You have a few minutes to talk about what you're doing?"

"Seems a little late to be asking, after you already started," I said, looking over my broom at him. "I'm not looking for attention."

"You gotta take what you want sometimes," he replied.

"My wife says the same thing."

"Smart lady."

The thought of another writer hanging out around the neighborhood provoked my jealousy right away. I think that tendency exists in all men, and I was in a constant battle with myself to keep that part locked away and hidden.

"I just graduated from Columbia Journalism School," he said. "I'm doing a series of pieces about the gentrification of Harlem. Folks around here say you're a big part of that."

"I'm not a big part of anything," I told him.

"You want to tell me who you're working for?" he asked, paying no attention to my wishes.

"For the first time in my life, I'm not working for anyone."

He wrote it down.

"Please, leave me alone," I told him, continuing my sweeping. "I have no need to be watched by anyone outside of this block."

But he wouldn't. He was young and in training to be a journalist, and had been told by some professor that he should pursue his subject regardless of what they said. The word *no* was not in his vocabulary. I admired the fact that he held true to his convictions so early in life.

He continued snapping pictures of me cleaning as I moved up the block.

"You'll miss the real story if you concentrate on me," I called to him.

"I'll make you the story then," he yelled back.

The block was filling out. The hotter the summer got, the more people flooded out onto the streets. The water pressure in all the buildings was low with the fire hydrants blasting all around. That was the story I saw, not an out-of-work advertising copywriter sweeping some street.

I finished with my last bag. The Reporter had been following me all day long with some screwed-up smile that was starting to mold into his lips. My day ended with the sun going down and the barbecues smoking up on the block.

Trays of ham, tortilla chips, and cubes of cheese were out. Pop Tarts were being eaten. Little juice boxes were being consumed. Sodas were gulped down. Similar scenes were taking place across the country. The drug companies were working on treatments for the ailments this junk was causing. Money was being made off the wrong people and the wrong places. I was sweeping as fast as I could, but I couldn't clean what was going inside the bodies of these children.

"Why don't you just write a story about these diets out here? How they are killing themselves with traditions that have been created for them by advertising companies?" I said to the Reporter. "It's what's needed."

"You're a symbol that people want to read about," he replied. "You're the story. You tell them!"

I was tired and went into St. Nick's for a drink. The Bartender knew my name and what I wanted by that point, which may seem romantic and comforting, but let me tell you, being a regular at a bar just means you're developing a convenient drinking problem.

The Reporter followed me through the door and sat down quick at the bar, ordering himself a Red Stripe to mimic mine. I had no need to rush back to the apartment, as Namuna was going through an interview and photo shoot of her own—though she was more than willing to take part in hers. She had clients lined up for months. The people from Dubai were offering top dollar for her to come back, but she said she'd never leave New York again. That she couldn't stand to be away from me that long. That there was plenty of work here anyway.

"Why not let me ask you a few questions so I don't have to make up the answers," the Reporter said after the Bartender put down two beers and took a step back.

He wrote in his little notebook.

"How long have you lived in Harlem?" he asked.

"A little over two years now. Moved here from California."

"What made you leave Cali? Do they still call it that?"

"I needed some shade," I told him.

"Do you miss the life you left behind out there?"

"I didn't leave anything back there. In fact, most of what happened in California are things that I would like to forget," I said, downing my

Red Stripe. "Why don't you ask me what you came to ask me about?"

"I see . . . All right then, why are you sweeping up these blocks out here?"

"I live here. I hate seeing the trash around. I want to have kids here. I don't want them growing up around garbage."

"Are you looking to start a movement or something like that?"

"I'm just looking to be clean."

"What did you do before this?"

"I was in advertising. I did nothing."

"You quit?"

"Let's call it a self-induced firing."

"So you plan on earning money just cleaning up the street?"

"No. I'm not doing it for money. It's for peace of mind. People don't really do things for that anymore. Thought I'd give it a shot."

"Don't you miss being creative?"

"Advertising has nothing to do with creativity. I work on my typewriter in the mornings for that."

"Want to tell me what you write about?"

"Only what I see."

"Is it about cleaning up the block? Perhaps my article can help you get it published."

"I'm not looking for that. I just want to get it out of me."

"All I'm searching for is a story to tell," he said. "That's what keeps me up at night."

We talked for a while longer, though it was mostly just talk of each other—where we came from, what happened before. History.

After we were good and drunk on his dime, I walked him to the subway station and wished him a good night. He headed back downtown to write his story while I stumbled up the block looking to get home to Namuna.

The older Chess-Playing Kid sat back and smiled at his younger sister after making his checkmate move. The women, getting bigger by the moment, sat wrapped up in their children.

I got home to find Namuna still in the midst of her photo shoot and interview. Assistants were smoking in my hallway. The camera lights made the apartment look different.

She was out on the fire escape getting her picture taken. The Photographer was clicking away, using the block I cleaned up as his backdrop.

"Baby doll, believe me when I tell you, this is going great," the Photographer said while snapping her. "I've done millions of these urban shoots and you are just amazing. Amazing!"

"Just be sure you keep the lights low so it looks authentic," ordered Namuna. "This is going to represent me to the whole city."

"My dear," he said, rubbing his forefinger over his manicured eyebrow. "When we're done here, the whole city will be talking about you. Now, you, assistant person, get some of those floor plans and put them on the bench by the window. A woman at work is beyond sexy. Beyond!"

I leaned out the window and onto the fire escape to fully see my wife, even though I knew I was getting in the way of the shot.

"Long photo shoot?" I said.

Her face lit up even more when I walked in, and the Photographer loved it. "Yes! Yes! That is the excitement I've been after all afternoon," he said, clicking away. I couldn't tell if he meant it or if he was just going through motions he wanted others to see.

"These people are driving me crazy," Namuna said to me. "It's more tiring than actual design work, which, by the way, I have to get back to."

"You know you love it," I said.

"It's a necessity for success."

"You look pretty comfortable to me," I said in the tense voice of a man whose ego was being upstaged by his wife.

I didn't mean it and was horrified that I'd said it, but my pride was speaking for me at that moment.

"This is far from any level of comfort," she snapped. "Don't you think I'd rather be alone with you?"

"This is your time," I said, not giving her the tenderness she needed in that moment of having to be strong in front of strangers. "I don't want to take anything away from you. Go on and enjoy it."

"With you on my side, I can enjoy everything," she said.

"You think I need to be at your side? That I can't make it on my own? Who do you think gave you the opportunity to be where you're at? It was me who worked at that fucking agency for how long? Doing this shit for how long? How many thoughts did I waste there?"

It was all coming up. I put all of my anger about my past choices on her. There was no stopping it. It needed to come out at a person and not onto the paper for once. Her face shattered slightly.

"Please, sir," the Photographer gasped. "You are absolutely ruining the mood. We were doing fantastic just minutes ago. Be a dear and take us all back to that place."

"Don't talk to me in my house like that," I yelled, trying my best to stake my claim. "Don't think I'm as patient as she is."

"I'm an artist trying to create your wife for the world. Please just let me work."

"Calm down, would you?" Namuna said to me. "This has nothing to do with you."

She was giving me an out, but being a man, I couldn't or wouldn't take it.

My body was turning against my mind. Inside, something was yelling at me to turn back, to step out onto that fire escape and enjoy the breeze up there with my wife, my strength—to live in that success that is so rare in life and have it marked by a photograph. That opportunity was being washed away with every step back down that hallway and drained completely by the door I slammed in the face of my happiness.

Alone in the hallway, the smell of smoke from the kids who'd lit up mixed with whatever grease was cooking in one of the apartments. I ran my fastest down the stairs to get out of the building and back onto the block.

I looked up to see Namuna still having pictures taken of her. She glanced down to watch me go. I knew I was wrong but had no spine to admit it. The fire hydrant across the street spewed water, and the kids who had been sitting on the stoop jumped in.

Their laughter was drawing me in. One of them walked out from the shooting water and made her way across the street toward me.

"You should try it. It'll work," the little girl said.

"I'm a little too old to be running wild through fire hydrants," I told her, managing the smile I could not give to Namuna.

"If you do, that woman up there might forgive you. All women have that inside of them."

I took her hand and walked across the street and into the streaming water of the hydrant. I cooled down. The sounds of laughter and screaming filled my ears. My eyes filled with water, but it was cool. I could see through my soaked eyelids Namuna looking down at me.

"That's where you belong, you know!" she screamed. "With the rest of the children!"

The Photographer snapped his camera. The caption would read: "Namuna yells down to the kids playing in the fire hydrants of Harlem."

Eventually, when the pressure died down, I would go back upstairs, but I let her finish and watched while the water blasted the chalk-drawn hopscotch game from the sidewalk.

2

Every store inside the city had sold out of air-conditioning units. Namuna worked away, as if nothing was wrong.

"How can you just sit there and work through this heat?" I asked, jumping up from the typewriter, trying to find another drop of water in the glass I had drained only a minute before.

"I just pay attention to my work, not what's wrong around me," she said.

"I'm not like you," I said in answer to the question she didn't ask.

"Maybe you have things to learn then."

I needed air-conditioning, so I left her alone, took the typewriter and hopped on the A train for some solace.

I tried to find an empty car, but the best I could do was score one with an old man wearing golf shoes without spikes and a few kids busting long backpacks, waiting by the doors to get off because they had just tagged up the car with shoe polish.

The kids exited on 125th, and the old man took a counter out of his pocket and clicked it three times.

I started writing and feeling comfortable on the moving, cool train. I figured that if that guy could sit there clicking away, my typewriter would be no problem. After all, it was portable for a reason.

There, underground in the shadows, I was in solitude and peace, away from pesky reporters and from my own rage brought to the surface by the summer heat. I guess that at some point, a man needs to be alone in order to feel comfort.

I should not have looked up. Somewhere on the edge of Brooklyn, right before I reached JFK, a stewardess trying to catch her flight was putting on makeup and getting her hat just right. There is something about a woman getting ready for work. She had an off A-line haircut and rimmed glasses.

"You going to the airport?" she said, not looking up from her compact.

"No, just riding the A train for the air-conditioning. Where are you headed today?"

"Off to Los Angeles! I do this flight three times a week. I've got a change of clothes there. Well, not really a change of clothes, just some beach stuff. I head right there each time I land."

"Doesn't it bother you to be going back and forth so much?"

"Doesn't it bother you to carry that big typewriter on the train?"

"It relaxes me," I said. "Most of the time I'm a kind of janitor."

"I'm a stewardess. Well, for now I am. Until I find out what my next step is. For now it's what I do, and I just love it. Kind of cool. Back and forth. Traveling everywhere. Crossing time zones. Like I'm traveling through time."

"What did you say?"

"It's like, I take off from Beijing and it's noon on Friday, and I get to New York and it's still noon on Friday! So cool! Even though I've been in the air for twelve hours, I haven't moved in time. Maybe I figured out the key to stopping it."

She smiled and winked at me like she wanted me to catch on to some joke, but sitting there holding the heavy typewriter with my pages stuffed under my arm, I wasn't in a joking way. I looked deeper into her face. Suddenly she just became another New Yorker who was late for work.

The doors opened and she went out, everything perfect. For the next few hours—those hours frozen in time—men would be stealing glances at her walking up and down the aisle pushing that drink cart. She was gone. Another story vanished through the doors of the A train.

3

Each night I walked up the block with my broom. The summertime was the best in Harlem because it was too hot for any nonsense. The flashbacks had stopped as I settled into my routine.

The block was static in its movements. Fire hydrants, radios plugged into lampposts, and the Chess Kids all remained unchanged. They were growing bigger, and their cheap little drugstore chess pieces had been replaced by the professional kind used by the old men in the park.

I was producing pages and cleaning up trash. I remembered how I used to spend hours trying to come up with four lines of copy, only to have it changed around by managers trying to make names for themselves, and then to be blamed when the client had asked for something that was more like what I had originally done. My eyes bled from those damn computer screens. I did not regret my decision once. I was becoming known on my block. It started to matter to me.

Walking up the other side this time, the St. Nick's side, the side that I usually looked across at, I could see things a little different. It always works that way. My stride was stopped by a man drunk beyond what is acceptable around here. "My horse. My horse just ran away. I have nothing now. Nothing."

The man was sweating at a rate that would suggest malaria.

"You said you lost a horse?" I asked.

"Not just a horse. My work. My life. My child. My wife. They will all follow the horse now, because that horse . . . that horse gave me the means to—that's what *I did*!"

He finished the bottle and tossed it to the street.

"Maybe you can call somebody. How hard is it to find a horse in this city?" I said. "They can't hide and don't have the money to pay a toll."

"Oh, you got jokes still," he said, and as he did, I recognized him as the man from the Laundromat who had asked to trade me shoes.

He didn't look too amused by my joke. I guess making wisecracks like that past the age of sixteen is no longer amusing.

He slogged up the block and vanished into the bricks. Behind me, the sounds of a couple in love shifted the balance of the scene altogether.

I turned around and saw an old couple holding on to their young voices. On the woman's arm, walking her proudly down the street, was a tall man who, although old in physical age, walked with the pride of a king because he knew that the most valuable thing in his life was not in his wallet or his book of accomplishments, but was walking right next to him. They passed, not noticing me. I saw the deep, dark eyes of the man in the reflection of the security mirror at the Chinese food spot that served noodles with ketchup.

4

The crowd gathered around Councilman Macon was fully enthralled with his booming voice, which carried well but didn't abuse the eardrums. He looked into the camera with every tenth word.

"Nobody realizes that aside from violent crimes, AIDS, cancer, and a general lack of consideration, one of the greatest killers of people in this city, on these blocks, is the heart attack.

"I was born on this block. I was raised by the same people who raised you. We are reflections of each other. It is my dream to nourish this place so that it may produce healthy generations for years to come. That is why I am heartbroken to find us participating in our own genocide. Snack foods and deep fryers are rotting us from the inside out, and we are paying for it! There is no need to round people up in trucks and march them into showers anymore. It can all be done with a McDonald's commercial now, and people will drive themselves there. Willingly! Well, I am not one to abide. I promise you this: As soon as I can, I will make sure that proper nutrition programs are put in place in schools so that our future has a chance. However, it is with you that this must start. It is you who must set the example."

His driver was parked next to the Chicken-and-Rice Guy and having a snack while his boss spoke and gathered votes. I listened as I swept.

When he was finished, he came over, bought the local grub, and took a bite that would get into the papers, framing himself as a community figure. He talked and listened to the complaints from folks on the block and promised that he would bring funding to the neighborhood he had grown up in.

I was impressed with his message and believed in what he was saying, though I thought he was a little short on solutions. It's never wise to trust a man who only points out the problems in life.

As the crowd dispersed, he walked over to me with a newspaper rolled up in his hand.

When he reached me, he unrolled it and looked at the picture in the paper, then at me. He showed me what he was looking at, pointing his rugged finger at a picture of me sweeping up the block with a headline over it reading CAN ONE MAN MAKE A DIFFERENCE?

"You are him, no?" he said in a voice that shifted gears from his public persona.

The Reporter had gotten his story published in the *Post*. In most cities, nobody is going to have time to notice a story on page thirty-two of a newspaper, but in New York, where people take the subways, you best believe that if something interesting has been seen above-ground, it's going to get talked about below it.

"My driver showed this to me."

"I'm not interested," I said.

"Not interested in what?"

"In helping you sell out the neighborhood. I've met people who work for you."

He laughed at what he wanted me to believe was the absurdity of my reasoning.

"These are my people," he said, cleaning off his forehead with one swipe of his handkerchief. "I'm attempting to raise their standard of living and bring more money into the community. It is for that reason that I've partnered with these real estate companies. Of course, there are concessions to be made. I give them a few town houses and they deliver me the large buildings where I can keep families safe and put in a few decent grocery stores that sell fresh fruits and vegetables. These are my children. I am their child. Whose child are you?"

It had been a long time since I trusted anyone as quickly as I did Councilman Macon. He saw it in my eyes.

"We can make this block clean," he continued. "Together, with your passion and my credibility, we can accomplish something magnificent. Let's go to my office and talk things over."

"Let's talk it over out here," I said, trying to gain leverage against my admiration for the man. "I feel more comfortable around these buildings."

The truth was that I was roasting out there and wanted nothing more than to go into the Town Car with its blasting AC, but I knew that I was about to enter into negotiations and I wanted any edge I could get.

"I have been sitting on these stoops for as long as I can remember—and that's a long time, my friend," he said. "So let this place serve as a monument to the first meeting place we share together."

He acted as if there were a million cameras on him even though we were alone.

"When I make speeches I enjoy drawing out my words, but when I speak business, I like to be direct. I hope that goes along with your way of thinking."

"It does," I said. "Although I'm not sure what kind of business we could do together."

"What I would like for you to do is to write out a detailed plan of what it would take to make this operation of yours professional. I imagine that if it were to work as a machine, with precision, it would produce fantastic results."

"I'm in no need of results," I told him. "I'm only interested in my process."

"So this is all about you, then?"

"I don't think it's really about anything. Just doing what needs to be done. Nothing more than that."

"Is that not a completely selfish way of thinking, of being?" he said while waving down a kid selling bottled water out of an ice chest he was dragging down the hot pavement on his skateboard. He bought two and handed me one.

The coolness of the water changed my chemical makeup.

"I just wanted to be a better person, that's all," I said, after I'd drained the bottle. "What's wrong with that?"

"I do not believe in looking at situations as wrong or right. The world does not exist in such ways," Councilman Macon said, taking only a small drink of the water. "What I believe is that everyone out there, at their core, wants to be a better person. You have an opportunity to make the situation better for everyone. You can achieve change. That, my friend, *that* is what is truly remarkable. It is when you do it for the satisfaction of others that you can achieve the peace you are looking for within."

He placed the almost full bottle on the hot step.

"You want to get elected, and you know that if you're responsible for a cleanup program it will play well," I said, trying to find a hole in his confidence.

"That is most definitely true," he replied, pleased. "I'll be totally transparent about that. But even so, I am satisfying a selfish need and still helping out the community. It is my need and desire for success that helps out those around me. Doing things your way only satisfies yourself. Where is the gratification in that?"

"In accomplishment."

"If accomplishment is what you're after, you could do a lot more with my help. Besides, it's your drive that will motivate others to follow you. Trust me, you remind me a lot of myself when I first started out in this business."

For children like me who grew up with a single mother, when an older man tells you that there is a connection between you and him, there is a huge void inside the chest that cries out to be filled. Those cries reverberated and made me feel like perhaps this man would give me the guidance I had always been looking for but was never able to find. I let my guard down and allowed someone to teach me something new. I never had that growing up and did not realize the empty space it had left until that very moment in the Harlem heat.

His smile was kind and unlike what I was used to from corporate America. The feeling of something not being right faded away, and I was filled with appreciation. It is a very difficult emotion to turn away from.

"I can see you are a man of vision," he continued. "You have something more, right? There is more to you than just one man and a broom. You can expand on this—create an entire plan of attack. I'm sure you can."

"If I did," I said slowly, "what are you prepared to do?"

"I'm prepared to make sure that your plan, your creation, turns into reality," he told me. "I'm not sure there are many moments in life when a person presents you with such a choice. I advise you to act on it. Look, I have the money to make it happen, and you have the vision to make my money do many positive things. Partnerships are created out of necessity. Believe me."

He patted my back and went back to his ride. He rolled his window halfway up and put on his sunglasses.

"Are we going to make this happen?" he asked.

My mind started racing over the resources that would be available to me if I teamed up with Councilman Macon. I thought of what I could build and how much of myself I could see in the tangible results.

"We are," I told him.

He smiled and handed me a cell phone through what was left of the open window.

"Good," he said, satisfied. "Give me a call on this when you have your plan written out. My number is already programmed in."

He rolled the window up the rest of the way, and his car pulled away, up the street and out of Harlem.

Looked like I was working again.

CHAPTER 11

THE BUSINESS PLAN

1

In the past, I had mapped out business plans for countless executives who, after smiling at me and telling me "Nice job," proceeded to take off the cover page and put their own names down.

Now I was creating a plan I was going to get credit for.

I was never much for believing that the universe sets up life for you, but when I started the plan, I had a feeling that everything that happened up to that point had been for a reason. All of the writing I had done in the mornings on the typewriter were just notes on the neighborhood. Those imprinted pages told of who the people were, where they shopped, how they talked, and, most important, what they wanted.

Those pages of thoughts I had collected could all now be incorporated into the plan. The training I received in the advertising world on convincing people to buy in was actually going to pay off.

I went to work right away. Figuring that it would be fast and more efficient to write it on a computer, I dusted off the laptop and put the typewriter away for the moment. Gathering up everything I had written, I started in and produced the following business plan:

THE "REP YOUR BLOCK" BUSINESS PLAN

TARGET DEMOGRAPHIC

It is imperative that we go after the youth. Specifically the age range of eight to twelve years old. Most older than that have already developed patterns and are beyond our ability to reach in this phase. The hope would be that the children we are targeting will grow into the next age demographic. At the same time, their parents still have a close enough eye on them to be affected through a "branding osmosis."

We can look at how the cola companies and chip manufacturers used bright colors and cartoon characters to create dependence. Once that dependence is created, there is no longer a need to market. The youth will start to seek out your product. Their minds will crave it. Our hope is that they will crave their neighborhood staying clean.

BRANDING

The brand will have to represent a grassroots campaign, as if it sprang from the actions of the neighborhood. We don't want to seem like we are creating something for the neighborhood, but more like we discovered the talent there and are making sure it is realized and not wasted.

To that effect, each member of the cleanup team will sport T-shirts with the same general color and brand pattern. However, each kid can design the logo he or she wants for the cover of the shirt. We can set up a simple online application for them to use. If they are not computer savvy, we can hold workshops that teach them how to use the application, and at the same time, we can promote computer literacy. The word will spread that you can create your own T-shirt, and more and more kids will sign up. Word-of-mouth advertising will serve the intended purpose here.

This will make it easier to hold fund-raisers, because most people, regardless of their social status, like the idea of giving money to help children better themselves. This touches on needs that were not met when parents and potential donors were children themselves and alleviates some of the longing for care and concern that may still be felt.

TAGLINE

Though the logos will be up to the individuals participating in the program, each shirt will carry the tagline REP YOUR BLOCK.

This will be the name of the program and carry the weight of all messaging. This three-word tagline will be easy for the children to say and evoke nostalgia in the parents.

IMPLEMENTATION
We are going to need to pay these kids to perform. Nothing gives a young man or woman a sense of self-respect more than paying them for a job well done. This will ensure the block stays clean. If a kid works hard at cleaning up their neighborhood, they are going to say something when it's trashed.

CROSS PROMOTION
Since the children are allowed to design their own shirts, they will be able to set up a Web page where they can sell those shirts internationally. With the words HARLEM, USA printed on the bottom right of the shirt, we can brand the neighborhood and the kids can start generating income from the sales. After money is subtracted from the cost of manufacturing and shipping, the child will receive half of the profit, while the other half will go into an account for neighborhood beautification.

The children in the neighborhood will have a vested interest in spreading the brand of cleaning up the block.

PERCEPTION
The whole campaign should appear to be run by children. Children inspire hope and will cause more people to want to be part of the project. Once the citizens of the block view this happening, they will feel as most do when they look at a child—free from the weight of adulthood. Free from the thought that it is impossible to change our way of thinking.

I put the whole concept down in less than two hours, loaded it on a jump drive, and made my way to Councilman Macon's office up on 159th just as he was leaving. His smile widened when he saw me running toward him, dumb-faced. Councilman Macon turned right around with me, and we went back into the building to work the business plan into a sell sheet that could be presented to his investors. All he had to do was make the right phone call and the budget would be in place.

"I'm going to do it on a grand scale," he said when we were done. "You should stand next to me when we announce it. It will be a great day for the neighborhood and one that you will always remember."

"I'd rather not be there," I told him, pushing away the empty boxes of Chinese food we'd ordered. "It's about the idea getting done, not me."

He smiled, rolled down his sleeves, and put his tie back on. Men like that could wear suits regardless of the weather outside.

"You realize," he continued, walking me to the door. "You and I are about to build something that will be remembered forever."

"That's all I ask," I told him.

"It shouldn't take that long to get the money," he replied. "Not that long at all."

"I still think moving slowly would be a better plan of attack," I told him. "There's nothing to gain by rushing into anything. After all, money is not the issue, right?"

"Son, when you are about to attack anything, moving at a slow pace will disrupt your momentum. Trust me, your plan is going to have the block looking as it should. As it once did!"

"You'll be looking pretty good yourself if it succeeds," I said.

"I look good no matter what. After all, I must reflect the neighborhood, and they must want to reflect my own success."

I walked back home down Broadway. I didn't need to walk, but I enjoyed those moments late at night, not having to worry about getting up for the office the next day.

A can rattled harsh against the sidewalk, and I turned around. I saw the Kid walking in the street not a few feet behind of me.

"At it late again," I said.

"I'm always at it. Got to keep an eye out for those who need me.

Looks like you already found yourself a partner, though. Word is that he found you. That right?"

"We're going to change things up around here," I told him. "Councilman Macon is going to put my skills to use."

"What is it you're trying to do?" he asked. "What are you looking to recapture?"

His laughter after he spoke broke my mood.

"What?" I yelled at him. "What are you laughing at?"

"You, man. I'm laughing at you because you have no idea what you're doing or looking for. You think you were at a business meeting this late at night this far uptown. The neighborhood hasn't changed that much, unless you changed it already, which I doubt."

"I'm changing it."

"For what?"

"To make it clean."

"I thought you were typing up there in the mornings to get everything out of your head. Now you're selling to Macon? Which one is it?"

"Why can't it be both? Why can't it be the same thing? Anyway, I don't need to explain any of this to some kid walking around the streets at night waiting for the sun to rise over the Harlem River."

"Maybe you're looking for a child to talk to. Perhaps you lost someone who you want to contact again. We all have our ways of dealing with that. Could be that's why you're so mixed up about what you're doing."

He paused as the sky lightened, hinting that the sun might be coming up soon. It always does. He continued: "If you watch the very thing that illuminated those bricks you love so much, you might understand what you are getting at. Or are you like everyone else— just afraid to know?"

I had no words. My skin was flying high off my flesh, and my bones were cold from his words. He marched off down the street and vanished into the almost sunrise before I could figure out what the hell he was talking about. I knew, though. Inside I knew.

2

I continued with my work. Hell, what did I care about what one kid was saying? There was progress to be made and I was heading it up. Something inside had been turned on since Councilman Macon decided to sponsor me.

I remember the day we opened the computer center at the storefront church. Councilman Macon had come through with the computers, and the Preacher had delivered on his promise to pay back the favor.

"You really are enjoying this," the Preacher said to me. "I can see in your face that you take pride in what you have done."

"I do," I told him. "Creating something in your mind and seeing it turn into reality makes you feel more like a man."

"So now you are happy?" he said, moving away from the stream of neighborhood kids coming in for the morning training session.

"Getting there," I told him.

"Just remember, accomplishment does not satisfy every need. That comes with family. Do not neglect that. Still, I am pleased to see the children of the block coming down off their steps and learning something. This will help them compete when they decide to leave."

Namuna walked up wearing a perfect summer outfit and a huge smile.

"Guess what I have to do today?" she said.

"Tell me."

"Nothing! I'm free, and I'm taking you to the park to lie down and watch the clouds in the sky move. We'll pick up a bottle of wine and some food and have a day of nothing for once."

"That sounds amazing," I said. "But today is the opening of the computer center, and after that we're signing all these kids up here for the Rep Your Block program. These are the people who are going to keep the neighborhood clean, and I can't very well just take off and leave them here."

"What am I supposed to do then?" she asked, which shocked me, because she never asked anything, she usually just did what she wanted. "You want me to go to the park by myself and watch the other families enjoying themselves? I'm not single anymore. There is no joy in that. Those are the moments when people are supposed to be looking at us."

"Well, you just had a moment when everyone was looking at you," I said. "Today everyone is going to be looking at what I created. That's important to me. Can't you see that?"

"I can."

"So?"

"It doesn't mean I have to be happy about it," she said.

"Happiness is not always the most important thing," I replied.

"What is, then?"

"Accomplishment."

"I agree with you," she said. "Only thing is that we are a team, so self-accomplishment shouldn't bring you the same satisfaction as what we do together."

"But I'm a man," I said.

"That, my love, is obvious."

With that, she put on her sunglasses and walked down the street, leaving me to do what I had set out to do.

Some of the women in the neighborhood, happy that their kids were learning and participating in helping out the block, brought down food for us. Councilman Macon stayed away for the most part and let me run the show, which was something I really enjoyed.

When you are a member of a company, you do your part on a project and rarely get to see it move through to completion. Usually you are starting on the next job, or at least your part on the next job.

There is not that satisfaction of seeing results. Here, in front of me, on the faces of these kids, I could see results.

Then, just as I was almost completely filled with joy, the kids who had been clowning me when I'd first started sweeping up the block came walking toward the church.

"Heard you were giving away some computers or some stuff like that," the Green Fitted Hat Kid said. "I mean, I'm down for that if there's any more."

"Not giving away computers," I told him. "I'm trying to give you the block. Why don't you and your crew come inside for a bit and you can check it out for yourself."

The smell of good food and sound of laughter were too much for them to ignore, so they slowly made their way inside to find out what was going on for themselves.

Granderson, on his way to school, stopped in front as well and looked at me with a tilted grin.

"You're making a lot of noise up here," he said. "You know what you're doing?"

"Do any of us, really?" I said.

"Some do," he replied. "Some do."

He continued on his way.

3

True to Councilman Macon's word, the money for the projects started to come in from his office.

Nobody I ever worked for let me have as much freedom as I had at that moment.

I had used some of the budget to buy a few new stereos that we plugged into the lampposts while everyone worked. We kept the volume at a respectable level, though, and let different folks decide what music came out from the speakers so that no one sound would dominate the scene.

Life was humming. The street was getting cleaned up, and the kids were branching into their own groups and creating their own methods of contribution. The two Chess Kids rounded up the youngins from their building and designed a collection of trash cans decorated by local graffiti artists. I put their thoughts into a request, and by the next day, Councilman Macon had twenty new cans delivered to the block. By the end of that evening, with the sounds of John Coltrane's "Blue Train" guiding them through the night (the Bartender's choice), the people of St. Nicholas Place woke up to clean pavements and trash placed inside of new works of art.

The Bodega Guy didn't participate and kept his music up loud most nights. He still tossed his butts on the ground, and his boys had no problems ripping off candy wrappers and letting them fall into the gutter. We cleaned up after him and he drew a few dirty looks, but his grip on the neighborhood and his store's necessity to it freed him from having to care. He stood defiant. Something would have to be done, eventually.

The sounds that had once haunted me at night started to quiet down just a bit. Councilman Macon was getting bigger outside of the neighborhood and was receiving much of the credit for supporting the program, which brought in even more money at lavish fundraising parties around the city. Sugar Hill was in the news again, and each time it was, he was there with a sound bite. The press was elevating his image.

In the past, the stuff I had written was part of the slow stranglehold corporate America had on its customers, but this business plan was changing reality. What work of fiction could have done such a thing? I had indeed made the right choice as far as what kind of writer I was going to be. True, I wasn't getting the face time that Councilman Macon was getting, but my sense of personal satisfaction had never been higher.

With the success of the first trash can program, the residents farther down the block asked for their own cans to be designed by their own kids. Though they all had different designs, just like the T-shirts everyone was now wearing, the tagline REP YOUR BLOCK was on each one.

I came home with my hands covered in paint and ready for some quiet time away from the street.

Namuna was on the couch reading the paper with an empty bottle of wine next to her. There were a few spots of red that had dripped onto the carpet.

"There's another story about the neighborhood in here," she said. "It's in the real estate section. EVERYONE'S GETTING SWEET ON SUGAR HILL! Catchy headline, don't you think?"

The sounds of sobbing from next door instantly shifted my mood. I went out to the fire escape and looked into Sukal's apartment to find her putting her life into boxes.

"What is it, Sukal? What happened?"

She handed me the letter that was the cause of her pain. It started by saying that this was her final offer, and that if she didn't accept, she had one month to leave the apartment. The building was going co-op and they had given her a buyout offer.

"I don't have the money to buy anything," she said through tears that were about to run out. "I'm going to have to move."

"Says here that they are giving you relocation money."

"Where do you think I'm going to relocate to? My life is here. The memories I created, we created, are here. Besides, it's not enough to move anywhere decent."

"They can't just toss you out," I said.

"I'll find somewhere to be," she said wrapping up some old highball glasses with gold rims. "That's not what bothers me. I'm old and can see the end of life anyways. But when I do go, I want to pass in this place we built together. I can still feel him inside of here. I'm with him here. Please, honey, you're going to have to go. Let me keep the boy for a little bit though, okay?"

"I understand. I'll let you be."

I climbed out of her window and back into ours. Namuna was waiting.

"It's great news for us," she said, waving a piece of paper that looked just like Sukal's in her hand. "They're going co-op. We're going to own this place. Oh, I can't wait to start tearing down these walls. I've got plans for—what, what is it?"

"Nothing. Just that Sukal is going to move out. She can't afford to buy."

"Really?" Namuna asked. "That means we can buy her place too. Knock down this middle wall here and have the entire place. It'll all be ours!"

She jumped into my arms full of love and excitement, then pulled back when she saw that I wasn't caught up in her mood.

"What? Aren't you happy we're going to own it?"

"What about Sukal?"

"I'm your family. You need to be concerned with me. With our future. With the future of our children, if we ever have any of them."

"So that's what it's all about, then. I knew you couldn't let it go!"

Her face sank.

"While you're out there trying to change everything around you from fools to gold, you might also want to take some time to look at me, your wife."

"You're doing great," I said. "You have everything you ever wanted."

"Everything I ever wanted is a foot away from me. You should feel the same."

I should have, but I didn't. Not then.

4

Back at St. Nick's Pub with a Red Stripe.

The woman I had met at the Laundromat was losing herself in

the music and a few bottles of her own. She noticed me holding my stomach.

"Ya know, when ya 'ave da upset stomach, jus' take a little salt and put that in a bottle o' Red Stripe and you'll be right."

She moved away, and I moved closer to the bar.

The Bartender moved in a slow amble toward each customer. Was he even walking or just being moved by one of those airport passenger walkways?

I wished that life could be lived like a song: short, amazing, and without too many words.

Granderson started the set with his trumpet. I now knew who the house players were and who were just musicians traveling through and waiting to sit in. There was a touch of romance to that—knowing the folks in the neighborhood spots.

A few of the older guys at the corner of the bar, who might have been there since the name changed, sat under the old magazine clippings that papered the walls while reading the present day's news. I could see Councilman Macon sweeping up the block on the front page, with a headline over him that read LOCAL POLITICIAN CLEANS UP HARLEM. A woman with a tightly cut, slightly graying Afro started talking to me when she saw that I was reading what the old men were.

"Harlem don't need any cleaning up, you know. We don't need any new heroes. What you think makes this place clean, huh? We've been fine for years. Neighborhoods go up, they go down, they get high, they crash low. There's no need to drive up the prices around here."

A younger woman, fresh from whatever office she had been working late at, put down her Absolut and tonic after a healthy sip and answered, "Nothing wrong with the change going on around here. Better food. Safer streets. I'll take that quality of living anytime. *Anytime!*" She finished her drink and motioned for the slow man behind the bar to fill up her glass.

"You think this is better?" the older woman blasted back, nursing what was left of her beer. "It's going to take all the flavor out of these buildings. Harlem is what its people are."

"These here are city blocks. What do you think you own? I don't mind being able to feed my children a meal that's not going to send them to the hospital with a heart attack in twenty years. Look at these kids out here eating nothing but those twenty-five-cent bags of chips from the corner store. Disgraceful."

"You can't go and call our culture disgraceful! This is our heritage!" the older woman yelled back, looking to take a last sip that had already been taken. "We've been living like this for years. I never want to give up how I eat. How I say hello. How my children can run from apartment to apartment and stay out late on the block. This here is family. This here is love. Why would I want to trade that in?"

"Because away from this block, you can't live like that. That's why when they leave this block, your children are having so much trouble. They can't compete."

"They can't *compete* anyways!" she said, rising up. "I'm not trying to sell out though."

"Those cigarettes you're smoking there, you know how much of that money you paid is tax to help the government? You better know what you're talking about before you go on about selling out. You're helping to construct your cell."

"Don't be telling me how to talk and what to think. Just because you got that suit on and have enough money in the bank to think about preaching, don't be bringing that in here."

"I've been coming in here just as long as anyone, and I'll—hey, what the fuck you listening to?"

At that point, they both noticed me listening in on their conversation. The two women who had just been arguing with each other took up adjoining seats and glared at me in solidarity, then continued their conversation in almost silent whispers, looking over at me once in a while to make sure I couldn't hear them.

My cell phone rang. I thought it might be Namuna calling to see where I was, that she might be worried about me, that she wanted me to come home. It was Councilman Macon. He called three times before I finally picked up.

"Things are going well. Better than I expected at all," he said. I strained to hear him over the drum solo. "Do you have time to meet?"

There was no hello. No greeting. Just the sounds of a man close to getting what he wants. Something happens once you reach that point. It is the lure of the obtainable.

"I'm a little drunk now," I told him. "Can we talk about this tomorrow?"

"Tomorrow? By then, today will be over. We should speak now. Look, I have some people coming down to the block around nine a.m. Do you think you can have the place clean by then?"

He was panting.

"I suppose I could," I told him. "But Saturday mornings I like the kids to stay inside watching cartoons and enjoying time with the family. Those are the best moments."

"It'll only be for this one time," he said. "Besides, the people who are coming, if they see what we've done, will want to give enough to help set up this program, your program, citywide. We can expand to help more people."

"I guess one Saturday morning wouldn't hurt," I told him, but as I did, I felt something inside of me tighten.

Each time you give in like that, each time you back away from something you believe in, a piece of you dies that can never be brought back to life. Don't let anyone tell you not to care. It all matters. Everything.

5

Right away, I noticed something was wrong with the morning sky. Usually, during summer in New York, there was a prevailing sunshine that illuminated the world in such a way that all seemed right.

The clouds moved quickly, then stopped over Harlem with an exaggerated halt. The rain started heavy and never let up.

Everyone worked feverishly, trying their best to keep the pots of planted flowers in front of all the tenement buildings from spilling over onto the block. They scooped out the gutters and used the falling sky as a natural hose to keep up their work.

Three Town Cars pulled up. Councilman Macon got out of the first. A few suits followed behind him. After the men straightened themselves out, Brenda Hamilton rolled out and dropped her shades. They all shook my hand as part of some ceremony while flashes popped. It was a very formal event, documented so these folks could show their friends what they had done over the weekend via email and Facebook. I hadn't reached celebrity status yet, but I was known by my kids, and they were known by their T-shirts, which you could now buy on a website designed from the lessons we were providing. The men walked up and down the block, and their photographer must have snapped a couple hundred photographs. Women hung out the windows to see what was happening.

"Do you want her in the shot?" their photographer asked. "Just the building or do you want the people hanging out the windows?"

Councilman Macon turned to Brenda Hamilton, who was running the whole show from a slight distance. She smiled at me, then turned her attention back to him.

"Sure," she said. "They help brand the neighborhood. When people read about Harlem, they want folks on stoops and hanging out windows. That's what we're selling."

Everyone laughed and wrote things down in little books. Some entered information into phones. Very soon, nobody was saying a word to me. I excused myself, trying to get some distance from all of them. Brenda mouthed, "Should have taken my offer."

"This is a fine, fine job you did here cleaning up," Councilman Macon said, patting me on the shoulder. "This block looks fantastic. I wish the sky would clear a little, but we can take care of all that in Photoshop. Everything can be manipulated."

He smiled.

The block was clean. I'd changed things. I'd made a difference. What else could I ask for? I kept telling myself those very words, hoping that at some point I would be able to believe them, though the same feeling I had back in the office, back when we were selling the Dominican campaign, started to creep in again.

The meeting continued, and I assumed the plans were being laid to "clean up" areas that were ripe for it all around the city. I walked toward home, up the silent block until a pounding rain fell all around me. Loud thunderclaps rang through the air.

Everyone took cover as quickly as they could. I looked back and saw Councilman Macon and his buddies duck into their Town Cars and race off. Brenda flipped up her collar and ducked into a doorway that gave her enough cover to light up a smoke.

The rain turned to falling ice.

I was alone on the block. The windows above were all closed. The moving trucks stood still. Tossed-out furniture started to soak. A few of the folks who had been pushing laundry carts made their way into the vestibules to wait out the storm.

And it stormed. Lightning shot out over the sky. Not quick. It was extended. Heavy. Loud. Weighty.

Car windows smashed. Alarms rang out. Even the ghosts that may have been moving around had no business being out. I quickened my pace, wishing that the stinging pain of the hail would make me feel something real.

At the top of the block, I could see the outline of a couple standing under a huge umbrella, kissing each other to stay warm, or to say goodbye just in case they fell victim to the lightning. Maybe they knew.

One of the trees blasted next to me, and I jumped, startled, into the middle of the street, where the last things I heard were the sound of a Red Bull can hitting the concrete and the screeching of tires failing to stop the boom that was lowered down on me.

CHAPTER 12

WAKING UP

1

Hospitals are nothing like Hollywood makes them out to be. We've all watched those scenes in which the person comes to after their accident, blinking their eyes wildly to get their bearings, and finally seeing the blurry lab coat of the doctor trying to revive them. Then there is a comforting voice to ease the patient into their surroundings as they finally get a grip on where they are.

Try this on:

My eyes opened in one shot. I had yet to be admitted into the hospital. The emergency room waiting area is where I came to. I could hear Namuna's voice yelling, only this time it was at the nurse who was handling all of the admitting procedures.

"He's been here for three hours!" she screamed. "The man is not even conscious. What are you people thinking here? Let him in!"

The nurse did not change the expression on her face. How could she? How much must she have seen at that hospital, sitting there running the show in the emergency room?

"Even if we let 'im in, which we can't be doing without 'im answering a few questions," the nurse said, "there are no doctors available to treat 'im. Just sit down and we'll try our best. Can't do better dan dat."

Other than Namuna's, hers was the voice that I recognized first. The woman from the Laundromat had made an impression that stuck with me.

She talked like she was reading from a telemarketing script. I had written a few of those back in the day as well.

Namuna walked toward me slowly and picked up her pace when she noticed that I was coming to. I guess I had been out for a long time. She smiled and brushed her hand over my forehead.

"How do you feel?" she said, looking at me as though something was really wrong.

As soon as I tried to answer her, I felt pain in places all over my body. My face felt like I had been shot with BB guns over and over again. My hearing started coming back, but that only meant that I could hear the groans of those stuck in the waiting room with me.

"How long have I been here?" I asked.

"Too long," she replied. "No reason to be waiting like this. I told the ambulance to take us to a midtown hospital, but they could only take us to the closest one. Said they had so many calls to take care of that there was no choice of which emergency room we could have gone to."

"I'm sorry we've been fighting lately," I told her, finding the words harder to speak than they were to think. She smiled then. It was a tender moment inside all of the pain.

"I should have been with you," she said, wanting to rub her hands over my arms but not wanting to do more damage to my bones.

"You're always with me," I said. "That's the truth."

They called my name.

Going between those two doors that led out of the waiting room and into the main hospital was terrifying. There, everyone's clothes were stripped off. Gunshot and stab wounds bled onto the floor. All the doors were halfway open, so you could get glimpses of what was happening in critical moments of people's lives.

The doctor came in and examined me. Gentle hands. They all have those hands—hands made for holding fragile pieces of glass. His face said nothing. My chest was pounding, as if my heart might break through what was left of my skeleton. "Well, I should tell you the good news first," he said flat. "That always helps."

Namuna bent over me.

"Whatever that man's about to say," she said. "Just know that I'll be with you through everything."

Her words were muted and sounded like she was speaking into a cup.

"It appears you've sustained a slight long bone fracture to your tibia. Though surgery is not necessary in this case, I would recommend it if there is nobody to take care of you at home."

"I can be there," Namuna said.

"In that case, he is going to require injections of Lovenox subcutaneously into his belly to prevent a blood clot. In terms of the pain, I'm going to prescribe oxycontin, though I would warn you about the hallucinogenic side effects.

"On a more serious note, I would say you're pretty lucky you didn't have a heart attack and die. You respiratory system is a little damaged, but with some rest and breathing exercises, you'll be back to normal soon. You may have to learn to breathe a little differently, but once you do, you won't notice the change. Habits are easy to form.

"The final piece here is that there was some damage done to your central nervous system. I'm not sure how much you know about all of this."

"Not too much," I said.

"Well, in layman's terms, this is what controls your speech, memory, and reflexes. It's your processing unit. There's a decent chance that you'll develop some problems with your balance and may have what we call 'blank spots' in your memory. My hope is that it comes back."

"I don't feel like I've forgotten anything," I said. "I still know this is my wife and that I love her."

"As I said," he replied, getting ready to see his next patient, "we don't know exactly how much is going to be affected. Most likely it will just be spots in your memory. Over time, you'll see. Now the pain, without the medications I've prescribed to you, might be too much. What I suggest is that you take them often but responsibly."

"I don't like pills anyway," I said. "Won't be a problem."

"It's not so much you liking them that I'm worried about," he said. "It's about you being able to deal with the pain you'll be in once they're gone. And rest assured that it is going to come. I can help you adjust to being at home, but you'll be on your own soon enough."

"You'll never be on your own," Namuna said to me, placing her hand on a safe part of my body.

After signing some papers and getting ourselves into more debt, we walked out into the cool Harlem night and took a gypsy cab back to the apartment. I had been forced to leave the regular goings-on of the world, and the fact that it had kept going without me made me feel insignificant.

I started to think about how, when just one number is taken out of an equation, the whole thing falls apart. It reminded me of all Robert's papers that were left in the typewriter case and how his calculations, if they'd been seen by the world, could have changed lives. His visions from the fire escape never reached the block.

When I tried to reach deep into my memory, it felt like the outline of a tattoo that had yet to be fully colored in.

2

I was at the window by the fire escape, trying to return to myself. The block below moved mellow with folks. A nurse came for the first few days to show us how to inject the medication properly, but Namuna learned quickly and took care of me herself. I think both of us enjoyed the stationary position I was in.

My phone was silent. The front pages of the newspapers kept talking about a new Harlem. A place where it was safe to walk around at night, with new stores opening up each week that were bringing money into the community. Most of the articles were advertisements in disguise, put in by Brownstone Restoration in an effort to get people to move into their buildings.

Wherever there was an article about Sugar Hill, you could be sure a picture of Councilman Macon was right there, smiling next to the words about how he "brought life into the community." Quotes from residents about how much they liked the new direction of the neighborhood shined on the page.

I could hear Sukal talking to herself as she packed her boxes and wondered what was worth bringing with her. She was almost done. Namuna brought me a cup of tea and took the paper away from me.

"How are you feeling?" she asked.

"Restless. I want to get back to work."

She paused. She knew that even though it wasn't Councilman Macon who had his hands on the wheel of the car that hit me, it was his pushing that had put me out there. She remembered his calls at all hours of the night, trying to keep me from sleeping and instead keep me working on what I thought was a plan for progress.

"All of this, most of what you see happening below," she said slowly, "started with you sweeping. It was your campaign, your business plan, your ideas that got everyone involved. Now those moving trucks, what's going on with Sukal next door—that was because of you as well. You didn't do it on purpose, but that doesn't matter. You did it. That's real. It doesn't matter that you thought you were doing something good."

"Looks pretty good to me," I said, taking a sip of the tea, wishing it was coffee, and looking across at the skyline. I knew I remembered the bricks and the trees up in the park just after 155th. How I could lean over the edge of the fire escape and see down the block as far as my eyes would let me.

Sounds of construction disrupted my thoughts. I looked down and saw a group of workers tearing up the street. Between the two buildings across from us, multiple families had gathered for a cookout.

I started remembering everything. I felt at home in each scene my eye took in. I remembered it all—everything about New York. But to me, New York was Harlem, and not just Harlem, this block. The stretch from 145th Street to 155th Street. I know that seems like ten blocks, but it was one.

Throughout the days of my recovery, the moving trucks came and went, emptying out the buildings I had spent so much time looking at. I had a feeling that the one across from me was particularly special, though I didn't know why. I couldn't put any faces inside the windows, but visions of being watched by a shadow flashed into my head.

"It's Macon," Namuna said. "He used the cleanup program to bring in investors for these buildings. Nobody who lived here before can afford to anymore."

"So it was me who made this happen?" I asked. "How?"

"You always could create campaigns to make people to do things."

"I just wanted to make a difference."

"You can't help what you are."

"I was just looking to show the people of the block what an amazing place they lived in. We just walk past most of it each day in the hopes of finding beauty somewhere else. We always look to the outside when it's always been right in front of us. I was going to be the one to show people that. It was supposed to be me."

"Well, now Macon is showing the world, and the world is taking this block from the people who live here. It was you who provided the blueprint for these people. You gave Macon your vision. Your desire to make a difference is causing destruction. That's just reality."

"I'm gonna kill that guy," I said. My head pounded. Namuna took my tea away and handed me a tall highball glass of water and two pills.

"Go on and take these, gangster," she said, smiling. "The only thing you are doing now is healing. I'm sticking around to make sure of that."

I popped them in and drank, then realized that the highball glass was Sukal's. Namuna saw that I recognized it.

"She thought it would help you recover faster," she said.

I stood up to take action but lost my balance and nearly fell out the window. Namuna closed it behind me and drew the curtains. Next thing I knew I was sitting on the floor in the living room with a glass of water shaking in my right hand. Namuna put five different pills in my left and told me to take them all, one after the other.

Each one that went down my throat stopped my mind from recognizing pain. After the last one, I wasn't numb, but I wasn't thinking of anything other than what was inside of that room. I hadn't spent much time in there. I started noticing our own pictures. Noises from the other side of the wall faded away as Namuna turned up the record player.

"Do you remember where we got this?" she said, bringing the jacket of the Miles Davis record over and sitting on my lap. She smiled at the memory.

I couldn't recall it.

"I don't. Was it around here?"

"No, no, this was before we moved here. When we lived in California. You remember that?"

I searched. I couldn't find that one. In fact, the earliest memory I had was of our van pulling up to the prewar building we lived in. I remembered everything about that. A little further back, I remembered pieces of the road from our trip out here.

But I couldn't remember anything before we moved to New York. I wouldn't.

3

I was taking more and more pills. The days were becoming easier, and the pain was not too much for me to deal with. Namuna was having trouble caring for both me and her own business. The magazine article had come out already and her phone wouldn't stop ringing.

I tried to get back into writing my thoughts down, to emptying my head, but usually I just sat there on the fire escape. I woke early in the mornings, while the block was asleep, and sat out under the gray morning sky of Harlem. How long would these blocks be able to exist like this? The bodegas were now being featured in Broadway musicals. Would the Chicken and Pizza spot at the end of the block be replaced by a KFC? Would there be an outcry and, more important, would it be heard?

The bedsheets hanging on the windows next door blew light in the morning breeze. Kids wore clean uniforms on their way to school. Namuna had left early to print out AutoCAD renderings for a carpenter she was working with.

Councilman Macon was running for reelection. New campaign signs showed his picture with the tagline REP YOUR BLOCK. The world I'd helped to shape was going on without me. The buzzer rang from below. Now this was nothing new. In these old buildings, the buzzers are always going off. Nobody really cares what apartment you're in, they just want in the building, and up until a few years ago, everyone knew everyone. The worst thing that could happen was to let one of those guys in with a food menu—sitting home by yourself during the day, you might get spooked by the sound of a piece of paper being slipped under the door. With the amount of pills I was taking, it sounded like a snake shooting in through the small space between the door and floor. I needed more Valium.

The buzzer kept going, and I drifted in and out of lucid thoughts. No. I wouldn't let anybody up. Wouldn't let anybody in. The voice started coming up from the street. A woman's.

"Let me in. Let me in."

It wasn't Namuna's voice I was hearing, but it was familiar. I buzzed up the voice and waited, then forgot what I was waiting for. The medication bent time for me. The doorbell rang out in excitement from hardly ever being used. I moved slowly down the hall while it continued to ring loud, echoing past me through the long rectangle and exploding into the living room.

I made it to the door. Maybe it was Sukal next door coming for

Knight. No. It didn't feel like that on the other side. I pushed down the little lever over the keyhole box and saw, standing on the other side in a wifebeater and barely there shorts, the girl from the building across the street.

"Aren't you going to let me in? I know your wife's not here right now. I saw her leave."

"I need to rest. Please, let me be. I never should have—"

"But we didn't do anything. We didn't. You should let me in to see how you're doing. I read about what happened to you."

She was waving a newspaper in her hand. I wanted her to go away, but I couldn't stop looking. She was a fantasy, and those are tough to come close to as you get older.

"You're not going to let me in now, but you will."

With that, she walked away. I could see high up her legs but not high enough to see everything. I was dying in that peephole. I couldn't help myself. I pulled it out and pleasured myself until she vanished from sight. I came and almost passed out fully by the door.

I made my way to the bathroom to shower off. I couldn't have the water on too hard, so I spent an hour with slow, cold water running over me, trying to wash away my fantasy before Namuna came home. I hadn't cheated. I never would on her. I loved her, but I was a man—an animal at that moment. She wouldn't understand if I told her.

The papers being read across the city told the story of a great man who gave up his job to make a neighborhood better. Those stories, the ones you read next to advertisements, never let the reader in on everything.

4

A helicopter circled above the apartment. Not that high at all. Somebody was about to get got. The block below had less hustle while the bird circled. The blades cut through the air. I had to get out from sitting in the apartment. Namuna and I went for a walk down by

Riverside Drive but had to pass the graveyard before we got there.

It had been what seemed like a long time for me since I'd passed the graves. A bird moved above us, circling once to see if we matched the description, then continuing its search.

The howls became muted from the graveyard under the chops of the blades from above. Sirens flew by. The helicopter followed them over the Macombs Dam Bridge and to the Bronx. Silence was renewed.

We got to the Hudson and just sat there.

"They want me to go away again. Beijing," she said. "Big development out there."

Namuna's words made the sun move down. It wasn't that I didn't want her to go and be in the world she needed to be in. Hell, I was happy and proud of her. My not wanting her to go had nothing to do with that. Would I be able to control myself, with all the free time I had? Would I start believing in ghosts again?

"Hey, where the hell have you been," boomed a voice not asking a question, but yelling in wonder.

We both spun around to see the group of kids who had once mocked me, and then had joined the Rep Your Block program. The Green Fitted Hat Kid still had a round gold sticker on the rim of his brim, though it was trying its best to peel away. They were each wearing the T-shirts that they had designed for themselves, though the shirts looked worn and in need of replacing.

"I've been laid up pretty bad," I told them. "How's the program going? Looks like you guys are famous."

"Famous?" he shot back, raising his cheek so that his eye was forced to squint. "Shit. We just got suckered. Cleaned up this whole neighborhood, and for what? So that we could move on out of here and make way for the downtown rats to come up here and fill what we helped build?"

"Babe, we should go," Namuna whispered. "No need to get excited on your first trip outside. Come on."

"Yeah, that's right, go on. Finish up with your selling us out!"

The others backed him up with hard stares. When I looked closer into those eyes, I could see the hardness break into sorrow.

"What do you mean, sell out?" I said passionately. "I gave up everything to make this neighborhood better."

"Better for who? That pimp Macon? Fool, either you've been played or you played us. Matters not 'cause the results are the same. We're moving out of here. Nobody can afford to live up in this anymore. Take a look at those moving trucks. Take a look at who's bringing things out onto the block and who's carrying their new Ikea shit up the stairs. We've been had."

I turned to Namuna and saw her looking out at the river. I flashed back briefly to her looking out over an ocean, then moved back to present time. The kids were waiting for something from me.

"Don't worry," I said. "I'm feeling better now. I'll be running the program soon, and we'll get it back to how it was. I'll make it all good."

"Ain't nothing ever like it was. You can't stop what's happened. Besides, none of us would fall for that again."

Namuna remained silent, as if she didn't hear them. It was like I was listening to ghosts speak, but they weren't ghosts, and neither were we. Just humans caught up in a game that was always being played. Even if you dropped out or got hurt, it never stopped. Never.

It was time for me to finish what I started. Namuna walked home alone past the graveyard while I tried to get back in with the kids.

CHAPTER 13

VOICES

1

Nostalgia was dangerous for me because it kept me from knowing exactly who I was. I had been helping advertising companies create ideas for so long that they had become my reality.

When I started the Rep Your Block program I'd felt whole. That had been taken away, and my contributions became mere footnotes to the movement.

The pills were altering me.

Sleepwalking made for disturbing nights. I couldn't distinguish between dreams, ghosts, and reality. I ended my medication after I had taken more than my dosage, and walked out the door and down the stairs. Though I was out on St. Nicholas Place for the millionth time, it felt like the first. Each step was a beginning.

I was under the lamppost, looking up at the glare and thinking it was the moon. It was late out—or early, whichever way you like to see the world. Around that hour, three a.m., when nothing should be moving and the people or beings who are only move because they have to. Maybe I had to be sweeping up the streets as I had done so many months ago, talking to myself continuously. There were very few lights on in the windows above. No sounds of children at all. Those pills were messing with my sleep patterns, causing me to sleepwalk all over the house, but never out on the sidewalk until that night. For the most part, Namuna could control it. She would guide me back to bed, but that night, I guess she didn't notice right away.

Someone else did.

The girl from across the street looked younger in the moonlight and without makeup on. Her hair was tied back, and she wore a pair of pajama bottoms that hugged where she had no panties.

"What are you doing out here so late? So alone?"

"I'm not sure. I just felt a need to do . . . something."

"You should come up for a little while, then. I can clean you up. Make you something warm to drink. Would you like that? We could sit on the fire escape."

Namuna had woken up and was leaning out the window looking at us. A gypsy cab slowed down, but the girl waved it away.

"Am I supposed to come up there with you? I . . . can't tell," I said. "I've been taking too many of these pills. For the pain. For the pain."

"Let me take care of you for a bit," she replied softly. "It's my turn. It is."

She didn't wait for me to make a decision and grabbed my hand, leading me into her apartment building. A voice screamed, "No. No!" Had I looked up, past what I thought to be the moon, I would have seen my wife leaning out the window screaming at me to stop.

I couldn't distinguish the voices I had created from those in front of me.

2

Somehow, I had gone back upstairs and slept all through the day while Namuna stayed awake, glaring out the window and across the street. What she must have been thinking. I needed some air when I woke up, so we went for a walk up to the park at the top of the block.

There were little flashes of light popping up from the grass. Children, a few of them, though none I recognized from the neighborhood, chased the lights. I didn't know kids still caught fireflies in jars. I guess up here they did. It was relaxing. The little girls walked slowly over the grass and selected the ones they wanted, while the boys tossed sticks and lurched out at the flies, more attacking than trying to gather. Namuna and I hung over the railing like we were at some ranch watching horses being broke. I was calm.

"We need to talk. I'm not sure you know what happened last night," Namuna said to me. Her eyes were surrounded by black rings of sleeplessness.

"I was out," I said. "Best I've slept since the accident."

While the children chased the fireflies, Namuna told me what happened. Though I shook my head in disbelief, perhaps thinking that the side-to-side motion would shake the straight line of truth, she kept on with the story. Stopping once in a while to gather herself and hold back tears, she made it to the end.

Inside, everything crashed to the bottom of my stomach, and though I tried to hold up the pieces, there was nothing to stop them from falling. There was no way to turn back time and fix what I had done. The pain I had caused her would never go away. The bond between us, the trust that holds a woman and a man together and completes that cycle was gone. It had been a sin. Now, I am not a religious man, but I knew when purity was broken. In all of the work I had done, of all the crap I put into the world, I knew that when I came home, what I put into my marriage was pure. It was right. It was love. There, in the park with the children trying to capture little lights that were doing their best to escape, I searched for a future in which the pain that was crashing around both of us might not be.

The little lights were popping up fast, and the sounds of little-girl laughter accompanied the motion. How could anyone know what was happening just outside their fenced-in sanctuary from the city? From adulthood?

"Are you going to leave me?" I asked, barely able to achieve a voice. "I wasn't conscious at all. I promise you that. Whatever happened wasn't me."

"I don't want to leave you," she sighed. "You have been so much of my life up until now. My love. It's because of you I'm doing what I want to be doing. How long did you work those bullshit jobs so I could work my way up and become who I am? But who am I now? Am I just another woman you lay down with at night? We've lost that sacred alchemy of each other. There is an impurity between us that can never be washed away. Never be replaced. Time may dull it, but the weight of the happening will always exist. Always."

She looked at the kids playing and rubbed the bottom of her stomach.

"It's just that before, when I looked at you, I saw only you, never anyone else. Now what? When I think or look at you, I'm going to see you and some other woman walking into a building together. Even if it wasn't your mind, it was still your body. You're not only mine anymore. How can I know that it's not going to happen again?"

A single tear that I hadn't noticed at first was moving down her cheek. It was the same tear I saw at the clinic that day. I remembered then. I remembered it all then.

"I'll stop taking the medication," I said grabbing her hand and putting it on my heart. "I hate what that shit is doing to me anyways. It can be like we are throwing that part away. We can try, can't we? What else can we do? I'd die without you."

"It's going to be painful without it," she said. "What about your heart?"

"You're my heart," I told her. "Those doctors have no idea. Let me try to take this memory from you so you don't have to wake with it every day. This time I can do it."

Word must have gotten out about the fireflies, because by now the park was full of kids and laughter, the lights of the bugs hinting at the

stars that were about to appear. She put her head on my chest, and we
sat there, watching the children play in the Harlem night.

I was back and ready to fight for everything.

Everything.

3

The low ceilings at St. Nick's kept my head from flying off. The
Bartender had on one of those old Cuban shirts that contrasted
brightly against his skin. I had never been to Cuba myself, but I figured that's what people wore down there. He wasn't looking right at
me, but I could tell he was watching.

"You thinking about doing something?" he said without his lips
moving much.

"How can you tell?" I asked, taking a drink of my Red Stripe.

"You have that look of a man determined to change the course
of the road he is traveling. For the most part, that's a pretty lonely
undertaking. You look pretty alone."

"I'm not alone. I'm married, though not by much these days."

"Doesn't matter who's with you physically. When you're looking
to do what you're about to do, whatever it is that you're thinking of
doing, ain't nobody can stand next to you. It's a hard time for a man,
because whatever he decides, he has to live with it. There's always the
road to look back on."

"What if I could stop and go back in time?" I asked. "What then?"

"Time never went backwards for nobody, so there's no use talking that nonsense."

He cleaned off the bar with a wet rag, using circular motions that
covered every inch of the wood. The action had been perfected over
great amounts of time.

"I've done the neighborhood wrong. That wasn't my intention. I
wasn't really thinking about right or wrong when I acted, only getting done what I thought needed to be done. I winded up handing

over power to Councilman Macon. I can't just let that stand. I was tricked, sure enough. I guess I wanted to be tricked because it is just another way to make life easier to live."

"Some things a man just can't change," he said, replacing the wet rag with a dry one.

"I know what can be changed and what can't be. Hell, this is not even top on my list of things I'd like to change, but it's the only one that's possible. So, as long as there's that possibility, I'm going to act on it, whether I have an army to back me up or not."

"So that's what you're looking for? An army?"

"It would help," I told him. "I've at least realized I can't accomplish what I want alone. My voice isn't enough."

At that he perked up.

"Armies get destroyed. We tried back in the day with the Panthers around here. Now they're just another symbol to put on a T-shirt or in a song lyric. What do you know about armies? You ever in the service? Me, I was on the boat going to invade Japan before we dropped the bomb."

"I thought there was no land invasion against Japan," I said.

"We were on our way. Man, I remember listening to the generals tell us that twenty-five percent of us were sure to die. Those were some nights I tell you. Made me regret enlisting, but back then, after Pearl Harbor got bombed, we all rushed to go and sign up. We were all part of the battle at that point. I remember—man, I haven't thought about this for some time—but I remember old-timers were all wearing their uniforms from WWI on the subways the day after. It was infectious. I got caught up in it. Tell you, though, when word came that we dropped the bomb and were heading back, I felt a peace come over me. Isn't that strange? All of those people died and vanished in an instant, and I felt a peace come over me."

He took his glasses off, exposing his drooping bottom eyelids and hollowed-out face, just like the beer barrel from the town house.

Perhaps that's what the artist was trying to get people to see. The vast amount of death—both thought about and realized—had never left him.

"Do you still talk with any of the men that were on the boat?" I asked.

"We all went on to live out our lives after that." He let out a sigh, then pulled it back in. "Once in a while an old vet will come into the bar, and I'll pour him whatever he pleases. No need for explanations when that happens. There's a look we share.

"Not many folks on that boat are still alive," he continued, looking around. "It's a miracle we didn't die right there. You best tell me what you're planning before you set out to do it."

"I'd like to take the neighborhood back," I said flatly. "Those same people are coming in, buying up the buildings, and trying to do to this neighborhood what they did around 125th Street. I don't want to see that happening here. There is a chance to save this piece of land. This block, at least. I know how to do it. I know my plans work. It's just that I'm going to make some enemies along the way."

"There are enemies to every cause," he said. "You usually just can't tell who they are until it's too late. Best to do something to bring them out in the open. Judging by the way you went about it the first time, you've already done that. Now what are you prepared to do?"

The door opened and the light of day flooded the pub. It was Granderson carrying his trumpet and bent over slightly from a backpack full of books. He put his instrument down first.

"How you feeling there, youngster?" his old man said. "School all you want it to be?"

Granderson went behind the bar, pulled out a bottle of seltzer water, and poured himself a glass. He looked at me and smiled when he saw what I was drinking, then turned his attention to his grandfather.

"Things are going well at school," he said. "Looking good on the internship, so next year seems to be mine. No time for my lady, though, which is hurting but not stopping me, you know what I'm saying?"

He finished his drink and put his backpack under the bar.

"This young man right here might be able to help you out," the Bartender said to me. "Though there's a chance I'm a little biased, seeing as how he's kin."

Granderson looked at me. His eyes were pure and clear, not bloodshot like my own. Focused. He was on track for sure and wanted no part of me.

"Yeah, I know you. You started this whole mess on the block. Got started out sweeping up and then got your funding. You were Macon's right-hand man. You want me to finish the job for you? Or pat you on the back to let you know that what you did wasn't so bad?"

"I don't even know you," I said. "Your grandfather is the one's been getting all the information from me. I'm just putting together a plan. That's all."

He didn't lift his eyes. "You have it written down?"

"No," I said. "I already gave all of that away. Give me a week to come up with something new."

"I don't have to give you anything," he said. "You're the one who needs me. I've got nothing but time."

With that, he started to practice his scales.

The Bartender moved back towards me.

"Don't be scared off by my grandson. He's a serious man. Needs to see that you're serious before he takes a step toward you."

"Before I can start working on anything," I told him, "I've got to get healthy. I've been so messed up on this medicine since the accident I can hardly see straight, much less put together a coherent thought. How am I going to get any plan together when my head pounds without the pills and swims with them?"

"I had the same problem when I came home after the war," he told me. "They had me on so much stuff that when my doctors wouldn't give me any more, I had to go to the streets to get it. Man down in Chinatown straightened me out. Been sober nearly thirty years now because of him."

"Except for alcohol, right?" I asked.

"Not a drop in that same amount of time," he smiled.

"You're not averse to selling it, though?"

"Man's got to make a living where there's a living to be made. Now, here, take this, go down there and get yourself worked on. Then you'll be straight enough to stand up and take another shot."

From his pocket he pulled out a stack of business cards he had rubber-banded together. He searched effortlessly until he found what he was looking for and placed it on the bar in front of me.

"Go on and see my man Dr. He. Pronounces it 'Huh,'" he said with a smile. "You won't even need to tell him what's wrong with you. He'll take a look at you—well, not exactly a look, but he'll be able to push out whatever ills are still inside of you. You better be ready for some pain, though, because it only takes one of his fingers to bring down the house. Best believe that."

4

Things seemed different downtown since I had worked there. Louder. Everyone was moving so much faster than I was.

It was around three thirty by the time I reached Chinatown. The kids had all just gotten out of school and were walking in packs. If you go awhile without speaking to anyone, the voices in your head start to determine the roads you take. Mine had taken me to the backstreets of Chinatown in search of a way to get off pills and back into the real world.

Dr. He's sign hung from an awning that had survived despite its age. Underneath it, three men smoked heavily in the heat. They looked at me for a moment and inhaled, one after another, like they had been drawn in an old Tex Avery cartoon.

"Excuse me," I said. "Is this where Dr. He is located?"

The man wearing an old Mets lid with an insurance advertisement on the side of it stepped forward and looked at me. As he tipped his cap, I noticed that his knuckle had a giant callus on it, almost big enough to be a knuckle on top of his original knuckle. I panned across all of them and saw that each had the same condition.

"We are the doctors," the man in the Mets cap said.

"I'm He. Please, inside, and I'll be with you soon."

"You all smoke?" I asked.

"Smoking not kill you," he said. "No. You can smoke too. Want smoke?"

They all started laughing at me and speaking to each other in Chinese. Dr. He took one last drag of his cigarette, choking with smoke and laughter, before flicking it into the dirty street and returning effortlessly to his work. It was a motion that was now a fluid part of his being after so many years of practice.

The place looked much more modern on the inside. A woman sat behind the counter with her daughter behind her. She took down my information and showed me where I should put my shoes. The daughter texted on her Sidekick, while the mother made sure I put my shoes in the right place.

A video of waterfalls played against a soundtrack of '80s R&B remixes. On the wall was a picture of a foot divided into hundreds of sections that corresponded to all the parts of the body. I was guided into the next room, which was dimly lit and made comfortable with a humidifier and the same video from the front room, only this time playing on a huge flat-screen TV. Four large La-Z-Boy black leather chairs sat in a row. At the foot of each chair was a small bucket.

"In bucket," the woman said, trailed by her still-texting daughter. "Put feet in bucket."

I did as I was told, and they left me alone for about five minutes.

By the time Dr. He came in, I had listened to a violin remix of

Boyz II Men's "Motownphilly" and half of a Sade song lip-synched in Mandarin. He moved my feet out of the water, dried them, and motioned for me to lean back in the chair. He looked up at me and said nothing, but his look told me that pain was coming.

With one swipe of his knuckle on the heel, the jolt from the bottom of my foot shot up through the tip of my longest eyelash.

"Back no good!" he yelled.

I screamed in pain but did not produce a word.

He moved to the ball of my foot and swiped again.

"Neck no good!"

The arch.

"Liver no good!"

"Knee no good," he said, rubbing his knuckle under my toes.

"Wrist no good!"

He paused.

"This will hurt, okay?" he said.

"It already hurts," I told him.

He smiled. "No pain, no gain. K?"

Before I could answer, he moved three knuckle swipes over the bridge of my foot. I let out a scream so loud that the woman and her daughter came in to check on me. The daughter started laughing and took a picture of me with her phone, and sent a text to all of her friends with the image attached.

"What's she saying?" I asked through my screams.

One of the other doctors who had been outside smoking was now watching the whole thing go down, laughing.

"Baby Foot! She called you Baby Foot!"

The whole place busted up laughing and saying the same thing in Chinese. I assume it was Baby Foot, which became my permanent name at Dr. He's. I felt my muscles relax and the pain go away for just a moment, until he started in on my other foot and duplicated the anguish.

Had you been walking down that street in Chinatown and

decided to duck into that doorway at that very moment, you would have heard the sounds of laughter, screaming, and chants of "Baby Foot" in Mandarin.

New York City.

5

On the train home, my feet were bruised, but my blood was circulating properly again. I felt each ache in my bones and a sharp piercing inside my head, but at least the pain was identifiable. Knowing that my body was regenerating itself had me believing in the possibility of recovery.

Across from me a mother and her child were sharing a moment of independence from each other.

The doors opened at 59th Street and in walked a man with sad eyes and an undone tie that just needed to be taken off. He looked like he made decent cash but had given up the decent part of his life to do so.

"Attention. Attention," the voice came loud over the speakers. "Due to a stalled train on the express tracks, all uptown A trains will be making all local stops. All local stops."

The few people on the train sat back, knowing that their normal bullet ride uptown was going to be a slow crawl. The man next to me started looking at the little girl across from him. There was love in his eyes for her, but not a sexual love. He was not a sicko. He looked like he had so much to give to someone. He made funny faces at the little girl, and she made them back, kicking the air in excitement with little feet that dangled off the subway bench.

"Mommy, the next stop is the museum. Can we go in for a little bit and say hello to the dinos?"

The mother was exhausted, but she got lost in the look of her child.

"I suppose that's why the train is making local stops, so you can see your dinosaurs?"

"I wish for it every day, Mommy, and it came true. Can we? Wishes don't come true every day you know."

The mother looked at the man in the suit, then at me, and smiled because she saw that we were waiting to see if the daughter would get her wish. Everyone on that subway car was looking for a miracle.

"I guess they don't," the mother said kindly.

The train stopped at the 81st Street station and the two of them got off together. The doors closed. The man in the suit looked at his mobile device to check for anything worthwhile, and then checked with me.

"I could have had that, you know. I chose not to."

"Could have had what?" I asked.

"A family just like that. I was young. I had my career ahead of me. She knew I didn't want it. That's why she did it. It was more for me than for her. I can't change what happened now. Still, it's hard."

He had started in the middle of his story.

"Whenever I see a child," he said, "I remember that day at the clinic. I was just starting to do the kind of work I really wanted to be involved with. I was building a decent portfolio. They liked me, you know. Only, I couldn't get any reception in that damn waiting room. It was before BlackBerrys or anything like that. I had a laptop I kept stepping outside with. They were very late calling us in from the waiting room. It took hours. Couples going through the same thing all sat around us.

"I kept going outside to get reception, a connection. The last time I came back into the waiting room, she was gone. She had gone in.

"I asked the nurse at the desk, and she told me to sit down. She was nice, trying to be calm, but she had seen hundreds of men like me before. We all had that same look on our face, like we weren't doing the right thing. It was then that I realized that I was not the one going through with anything. It was her in there, facing it alone. About to destroy something inside of her. To get rid of it.

"Time crept forward. I had already gotten my work done and approved. They were happy with me and leaning towards hiring me on full-time. With the money they were offering, I could have afforded a family right then. Maybe I should have rushed in and stopped everything. I didn't have the ability to make a decision. Or maybe I did, but I couldn't. I'm still haunted by that moment, among others.

"The door finally opened and the nurse told me I could go in and see her. She was wrapped in a blanket and asleep from the drugs. She turned over to look at me, a single tear rolling down her cheek.

"That image still haunts me."

The train stopped at 125th and he stood up to leave.

"Thank you for listening," he said, vanishing out into his stop as the train continued up toward mine, now running express again.

The train was empty and felt like it had been that way for some time. The mother, daughter, and man had all shared their history with me for just a bit, and though they had vanished along their own paths, we were all going to the same place.

CHAPTER 14

THE FIGHT

1

I knew that in order to write the plan this time, I would have to come down from the fire escape and sit down right there on the streets. The antiseptic offices that I had escaped from could not produce the work I needed to do, nor could writing from far above everything. No, if this was to be a movement that came from the people of the block, I would need to have their voices put into it. The truth is that it was their block, not mine. They had been born here. They had lived here. Loved here. Died here. Bled here. Been burned out and forgotten. Been judged and tried without voices of their own. Perhaps all they needed was to be left alone, but the world was not going to do that.

I knew from working inside those offices that there was no way valuable real estate was going to be left alone. I still thought like that. I couldn't shake it out of me, but I don't think I wanted to. I was happy about the man I was and what I had achieved in one world. I knew that I would be able to carry it over into the next. What was getting at me was that I had been defeated. I let someone get me— best me at my game. That had never happened to me before because, to tell you the truth, not only was I the best in whatever I did, but I knew I was the best.

That was a different time. This project required that I take all of the voices from the block and create a plan that they could carry out. I think one of the biggest problems executives have is that they sit in their offices, think about what would make *them* happy, and then carry it out using *their* ideas. That is why the market these days is ruled by such nonsense. People with those jobs are striving for the absurd and ironic. They are searching for the humor in their lives and want the irreverence they feel toward their jobs to be marketed in the form of ideals.

In order to have true and lasting control, like Norman Rockwell did—like all the masters who shaped reality did—I needed to create the world for them based on the lives of their dreams.

With Councilman Macon holding on to the money, I had answered to him. I'd handed everything off to him. Now I was getting back to my original vision and not letting anyone take any part of it away. I was sure I would be able to rally everyone around it this time, to protect what was left.

With some of the furniture that had been left by the people who had been forced to move, I set up a small office right out there on the block. Using the typewriter and a few candles for when it got dark, I didn't have to depend on electricity. I used an old Snapple bottle as a paperweight for the pages I was producing. It felt right to be typing away again.

For the most part, everyone left me alone. Armando took out the trash from the building at the end of each night, and as he did, he just looked and smiled, not really caring what I was doing. He was too busy to worry about anyone else, and as long as they weren't messing with his buildings or trying to take any of his daughters away, he was cool with almost anything.

The Preacher, sometimes returning from his sermon, and sometimes walking his wife from her ride on the A train, would tip his hat to me and ask if I wanted to join him for some bird.

Best of all there was Namuna. Although I am sure she did not like the fact that I had chosen to go back to this fight, to this plan, she still sat with me, editing my notes and adding her commentary when she could. She was working through a few projects of her own but needed the space and comfort of upstairs, so she remained there with her modern devices, calling for me when it was time to stop or just coming down with some wine in a coffee mug.

Crossing Guard Lita smoked out of her window and watched over the block. She would call the police on the Bodega Guy, but when they came by, he just leaned into the car and after a few minutes, the cops had gone. His music stayed on full blast.

She came up from behind me and exhaled her cigarette over my left shoulder.

"Boy, you've been making noise out here for nearly a week and haven't told me what you're doing," she said. "How long do you intend on keeping it up?"

"Until I'm done," I said. "Hey, I hardly recognized you without your bat."

"Gave that to those kids playing ball down at the pool. Don't try to switch the subject on me. What are you doing out here?"

"Coming up with another plan for the block," I told her. "One that doesn't involve Councilman Macon."

"Hey, Pop!" she yelled into the window. "This boy out here thinks he can still change the world."

"Well, let him go and change it then," a voice boomed back. "Makes no difference to me."

The sounds of the typewriter gradually brought more and more people on the block over to see what I was doing. I made no attempt to hide anything. I wanted them out there and involved. Though they were my words, it would be their voices that would help decide the future. My place in the history of everything, of the stories that were told, would be that of the man who brought everyone together and then faded away. In the first phase, I had imagined myself as just a man with a broom on the block, but this time around, I would be something more.

The pace of the keys hitting the page controlled the rumble of the people and the tempo of the chatter. Soon everyone started to read as I wrote and make edits right on the spot. I became more of a transcriber at that point. When something wasn't right, they shouted out.

"No, that's not true," said the woman coming back from her shift driving the M60 bus. "If we grow vegetables around here, the mice are going to come around even more."

"Woman, you have no idea what you're talking about," replied the Poland Spring Water Delivery Man, while eating the chicken and rice he bought from the van down the street.

"Don't tell me I don't know!" the woman said. "I'm from Georgia, and I *know* about growing vegetables."

"I knew you was country by the way you make a point," the man said, loosening his tie. "You keep that in there, son. We can work around it. Growing your own will work just fine."

A young teacher rounded the block and happened upon the gathering. Though she was struggling not to drop her huge folder of papers to correct, she still stopped by to check out the scene.

"Why not just use a bunch of cats to keep the mice away?" she said. "Sure the ASPCA wouldn't mind if you took them off their hands. You'd have to get them fixed first, of course. That way you could get some funding and support from all the animal rights groups."

"That's the stupidest thing I ever heard," said a nerdy girl wearing glasses, who would be unable to hide her curves in a few more months. "Sounds like the start of a bad fairy tale if you ask me."

"Ain't nobody ask you, book beast," the Green Fitted Hat Kid said.

"Well, you were asking me for more than you could actually take last night, remember, Mr. Early Riser?"

The entire crowd busted up laughing at that one, and I just kept typing away. The Green Fitted Hat Kid slumped down and walked away while the Nerdy Girl smiled in victory.

"No cats," she said, eyeballing Chicken Bob, who had taken up a post just outside the circle of commotion.

On it went and on I went. Shifts changed, and people heading to work and getting off work and looking for work all stopped by until their voices streamed into one.

I was up early each day and saw the Chicken-and-Rice Guy setting up down the block. Late in the afternoon, once he was sold out, he would come up to me and look over where he fit into the plan.

"You can keep the money in the community if everyone buys food from each other," he said. "Or trades. That worked out well, what you did for the Boxer. He's much more of a man these days."

That was the thing about letting everyone know you were writing about them, but this wasn't a story or anything so self-indulgent as that. It was just a plan to make all of our lives better, and once everyone started to understand that the community was made up of each of them, that they each had a role in its development and say-so over the course of their lives, they wanted to be a part of it.

When the man who cleaned the cars with the hose and heavy buckets of water he carried out to the street finally made an appearance, I knew I was reaching everyone. He was out there most every day of the year, through the blazing summers and into the winters when the wind made it painful to walk. Only snow slowed him down, but not by much.

"We see each other all the time," he said, wrinkling his nose and holding firm to his stare at me. "We're cool with each other, but you know, I've been here since I was a sprout. I've seen these kids piss on the block. I've seen the block swallow them up too. If you really want to get at them, you're going to need to give them a foundation. You're going to have to hand control over to their parents. In order for their parents to have control, they're going to have to have money. Real money. Money generated by the community."

"You're talking about fund-raising," I asked him. "Like a fair or a block party, something like that. You want me to put that into the plan?"

"I'm talking taxes, man. Real government. We need to have the community generating money that gets put back into the block. That way, our hand isn't out to anyone else. We can support ourselves."

"What are we going to tax?" I asked.

"That all depends. I mean, I make a pretty decent amount on my business right here. I don't flash a lot, but I do all right and I own my own. Even the Chicken-and-Rice dude, he does great. I wouldn't mind giving something back as long as I saw some returns from it."

A classic '64 rolled up and he went back to work. So did I.

It didn't take long for people to come around with their own pieces of paper, diagrams, and suggestions. My table became stacked with pages, napkins, and whatever else could be written on.

After the last suggestions were given, after it all ended, there was silence.

Namuna came down and put her arm around me.

"I can feel Councilman Macon out there," I said, not looking at her. "I hear him breathing."

Crossing Guard Lita walked out in front of us, now wearing her normal gear. Her dogs panted heavy in the heat.

"My father says there used to be awnings to protect us from the sun beating down like this," she said, pulling her dogs back from pulling her.

"You tell him that's the first thing we're going to put back in place," I said.

She looked deep into my eyes as if she were looking for a soft spot, and smiled when she was unable to find one.

"When that day comes," she said. "You'll see us taking walks together."

"What a day that will be," said Namuna. "If I could have just one more walk with my father, I'd consider my life just a little more complete."

I went to put my arm around Namuna, but it cramped up on me, sending a strong pain shooting down my back.

"Is it worth it?" she asked. "I thought that by now, after everything that's happened, you might start looking out for yourself just a little bit."

"I am looking out for myself," I said. "This is who I am."

We walked back upstairs together, and I used the last energy I had to brew a pot of coffee and gather everything the neighborhood said and put it into a cohesive plan.

2

Granderson had a copy of the plan and liked what he saw, at least enough to put the word out on the block that I was worth listening to. He handled who would be attending, making sure that the decision makers of the neighborhood were going to be there. No politicians, no police, and no media. We were out to get something accomplished, so it had to be done in secret.

The Preacher agreed to let us set up a barbecue for all the people in the neighborhood in front of his church to serve as a cover for our block meeting. He took advantage of the large gathering to boom a special sermon from his sidewalk microphone, its chord running through the lamppost outside.

Behind a door in the back of the church was a waiting area that led up to a room above the sports bar. At varying times in the life of this building, this had been either a secret entrance or an escape route.

Granderson decided which people were cool to come into the back room through the church. Each time the door opened, you could hear bits of what the Preacher was yelling but could only understand it if you spoke Spanish. A few kids in the back row adjusted their ties while the lucky ones got to practice on the drums and piano.

The room filled quickly, and as it did, we started letting people upstairs. The second Brand Nubian album played softly in the background so those arriving would feel like they were marching out to a title fight as they ascended. The leaders of each stoop crew showed. The Boxer leaned against the wall. The old couple that took nightly strolls whispered into each other's ears. The Chess Kids even stopped their games to come and listen. Granderson closed the door behind him as he went in, not leaving me enough room to enter.

"I'm not sold on you just yet," he told me. "But I like the fact that you don't accept being beat. You've got my ear for now, and if you've got my ear, then you've got the block's ear. What remains to be seen is what you do with it."

"How are you not going to let me in there?" I asked. "I have to be a part of this."

"You are," he said, not letting his eyes move. "But if you get up in front of all these people and tell them what to do—no. No, that's not going to work. You can't be the face of this movement. You've done your part. It's known."

"I don't care if it's known," I told him. "I just want to be inside when decisions are made."

"If you come inside and start reading this plan, nobody is going to hear you. They are good with you writing it. With you helping to give it shape, but you can't be the one who yells 'Charge!'"

"So what am I supposed to do now?" I asked, exasperated. "Just sit out here and wait?"

"You have a wife, right? Go home to her. That's what you should be begging to do anyway, not to get up and speak in front of a bunch of people who have never said the words 'I love you' to you."

He put his hand on my shoulder and tried to think of the perfect words to say but couldn't find them. He pulled his arms back, closed the door, and I heard him walk up the stairs. I walked back out to the sounds of the Preacher booming on the sidewalk, unable to understand a word.

It was time to go home. The next day would bring decisions.

3

"How're the Chinatown treatments going?" Namuna asked.

"Painful but good," I told her. "I like not having those pills in my head anymore. I can see all of you, and feel you, like before."

I could tell from her breath and the half-empty bottle of wine that she'd been out there for a while.

"The meeting's over already?" she asked.

"No. Granderson thought it better I was heard but not seen."

"That makes sense to me. Kind of like how it's been between us lately. A woman has to come down to the block to meet her man. That's not how the love story is supposed to go."

"I never was one for writing a good story of any kind," I said, filling a glass and sitting next to her. "But I can write a business plan that changes the world."

"And by change you mean almost destroy it?"

"Well, that's kind of a change, no?"

She was drunk enough to laugh at my humor, and her smile was enough to make me happy.

"The neighborhood is calm tonight. Notice how quiet it is?" she said, emptying the rest of the bottle into her glass.

"Everyone is planning for their part," I said. "Or at least wondering if they even want a part in it. Let's not talk about any of that tonight. You're leaving so early in the morning."

I leaned in to kiss her. Our lips touched, but I could feel her pulling away, though she kept up the motions. Her body was there, but her soul, some percentage of it, was somewhere else. I opened my eyes slightly to watch her, only to find that her eyes were fixed on the window across the street. Or more important, on what was inside that window.

"What are you looking at?" I asked. "There's nothing over there. Nothing."

"I'd like to feel that—that there is nothing over there. That your body had never been deep inside that window. That I know what is behind those curtains and don't have to imagine the floor plan, or what the place might look like. That there isn't a mysterious part of you that I will never know. That some piece of your history doesn't belong to someone else."

"We both had histories before each other," I told her over my glass.

"Yes, but when we got married, our paths were to be one. That's what you said to me, right? 'We will create our own road to travel down, so that when life delivers the unexpected, we can change direction and map the world as we see it. As we want it to be.' That's what you said. That's what you wrote to me. But that woman—and I do see her from time to time—had no business being in on what we created. I don't have room for that."

"Does that mean you can't kiss me anymore?"

"I don't feel it in the same way. Perhaps during the time apart, with me working so much and missing you, I'll be able to create space to love you like I used to. But for now I can only kiss you like this."

The planes above momentarily drowned out the noise from the Bodega, but passed quickly, and the music resumed blasting at full volume.

4

I was nervous waiting for Granderson at the Chicken and Pizza spot. I'd had two cups of coffee already and was trying to calm myself down by watching Chicken Bob scour the floor for any pieces that may have been missed in the early cleanup. Through the window, I saw Crossing Guard Lita walking her dogs, the Bus Driver walking back to resume her route, and the Schoolteacher racing to make sure she wasn't late.

Across the street, the Nerdy Girl and the Green Fitted Hat Kid stood together as the school bus came slowly down the street. She walked up the stairs, and he let her go, and, once she couldn't see him, watched until he couldn't see the bus anymore.

Granderson walked in, his pace quick. His eyes looked heavy, like he hadn't slept at all.

"I think you're going to be happy with what I have to tell you," he said. "We didn't break out of there until three a.m., but nobody wanted to leave until it was all worked out."

"Did they go for my plan?" I asked, finishing off my coffee while he ordered his.

"First off," he said, ripping into an egg-and-cheese roll he had brought with him, then waiting to finish until the bite was stuffed into one side of his cheek. "You can't think of it like *your* plan. It is *our* plan. Something we did together."

"If we did it together," I said, "I should have been able to come in last night and deliver it."

"The point is that we are going through with it."

"We are? Why didn't you just say that to start off with?"

We moved to sit down by the window, and he went over the entire meeting.

"The thing is," he started, "Nobody was surprised by any of what was in the plan because it contained the voices of the people of the block. They'd heard it all being said for years, and in the days you were putting it all together, but then when they heard me reading it up in front of them, they felt, I guess, *immortalized* in some way. They knew their thoughts were being taken into consideration."

"That never occurred to me," I said. "I should have known to play on that. It worked anyway."

"Your ability is there, man," he said. "But your way of thinking is messed up."

"That's how I was trained. Anyhow, what're the next steps?"

"What we need to do first is get pictures of all the real estate agents on the block. We have to know who they are. Do you know anyone with that kind of information?"

"Not directly, but I know someone who knows how to get it."

The thought of bringing the Reporter back into this upset me. It was because of him that Councilman Macon got involved in the first place. But the focus now was on getting the job done the best way possible. He was young enough to throw himself fully into this cause. That, and having the inside track on a feature story, would appeal to him. I'd pitch it to him like he was going to be Hunter S. getting in with the Hell's Angels, though this was a more socially conscious undertaking.

Granderson finished his coffee and stood up to go.

"Come on," he said. "Walk with me to the train and we'll go over the rest. Besides, I want everyone to see you walking with me."

So we walked back down St. Nicholas Place together and continued talking. Each of the people we walked by had their own connection to the plan.

"These stoop kids here are going to make sure that nobody else comes up and takes these apartments. Once they get to know who the agents are, they'll follow them and do what they can to disrupt any new people from moving in.

"All of this trash you see on the street is going to be gone. The supers can take care of it in the morning, but in the afternoons, we're going to hire out those same kids as before to clean up the block. Instead of getting the money from fund-raisers, we're going to get it from the block. Anyone who sells anything here is going to attach a tax to it. That tax money is going to pay the kids.

"Thing is that right now all we have is the car wash and the Chicken-and-Rice Guy selling on the block, so what we're going to do is get these people out of their houses and start them selling things right here. Different foods, sewing services . . . even the gypsy cabs are going to be taxing folks. Nothing big, just an extra twenty-five cents a ride. In turn, they'll be able to service this block and make money off of the people living on it.

"The biggest get for us is the two gas stations. That was a great idea on your part, I have to say. What we decided was a three-cent tax on each gallon of gas. That money is going to go directly into a fund to help people buy their apartments or cover any rent increases. Over the next few years, if you figure it out, we might be able to start buying the entire buildings ourselves. Nobody is going to notice a few cents on a gallon of gas."

By the time he reached the subway on 145th, he had laid out the basics of what everyone had agreed on.

"How are you going to enforce all of this?" I asked. "I mean, ideally it works. What makes you think you can implement everything?"

"You asked for an army. This block is full of soldiers who know how to run operations efficiently without drawing notice. Don't worry about that."

We both paused and looked back over the concrete we had just walked down.

"What's my part in all this?" I asked.

"You? You're going to be writing the campaigns for each of these movements. You'll be the marketing genius behind it all, but you'll have to stay behind it all for it to work."

"And you?" I asked.

"I'm the face."

He checked his watch, shook my hand, and flew down the steps and off to school.

There was no mention of Councilman Macon, so I figured he would have to wait. He would come out soon enough, when he felt any bit of power eroding from his grasp. You can't just go in and cut the head off the monster. There are steps to take. There is always a process. A system.

5

The Reporter had come through with pictures of all the real estate agents who rented out apartments on St. Nicholas Place between 145th and 155th. When one of them would meet a potential client, we started in.

A normal routine was for two kids riding dirt bikes with no brakes to speed past a young couple, one of them snatching a purse.

They would yell out well-rehearsed lines like "Shit is going to happen each day you walk down this block" or "Best keep to what you know."

They'd then toss the purse into the middle of the road and take off down the street laughing. The young woman would run after her purse, with her boyfriend following after her. They wouldn't be back. The scheme was repeated until word of mouth got out, and the brokers would be left standing in front of buildings, waiting for appointments that were never kept.

I thought this created a bad image of the neighborhood to the outside world, but Granderson didn't care what anyone outside the block thought.

"That's none of our concern," he said. "Let them think what they want. They're going to think it anyway. Besides, over time, as the neighborhood comes under our control, those same people who are judging us are going to be wondering how we took charge and turned the block around."

"What about Councilman Macon?" I asked. "There's no way he'll stand for it."

"He'll be looking to put a stop to it, that's for sure," Granderson said. "However, he's going to do his best to keep it out of the papers. If word gets out to the mainstream about the neighborhood being too dangerous a place to live, all of those properties he's buying up through that real estate company are going to drop in value. You can bet that he'll come to us for a deal. To *you* for a deal."

The plan continued throughout the week. Sometimes we'd have people meet the newcomers at the top of the stairs to "welcome" them to the neighborhood.

6

I remember the Fourth of July that summer—spending it at St. Nick's, waiting for Namuna to get back from her trip. I remember feeling that although both of us were in the middle of doing what we considered to be great things, all I wanted to do was hang around at home on a lazy Sunday afternoon.

I saw one of the brokers we had targeted sitting up at the bar, unshaven and looking glum, searching his pockets for enough to buy just one more beer.

"Can I help you out with that?" I said, suddenly realizing that I was responsible for his present state.

"Thanks. I'll get you back at some point," he said with his head down. "Business has been really bad lately. Usually, this time of year, I'm making g's. Not now though. Seems like someone is just out to get me. This neighborhood was turning. I mean, we were about to turn it."

The Bartender brought him a beer.

"Maybe you're associating with the wrong people," I told him. "The universe has a way of delivering karma."

"How's that?" he replied, stopping the beer from reaching his lips and putting it back on the bar with force enough to raise an eyebrow from Granderson, whose eye was on me from the stage.

"I'm just saying," I said, trying to be easy, "I see all of those trucks moving people out of the buildings at just about the same rate as your clients are moving in. You know what I mean?"

"How the hell do you know me? Know what I do?" he asked. "You watching me?"

He was drunk, angry, and getting poorer every day—a combination that had ruined many men. He grabbed the arm of a woman walking by him, who was giggling on the arm of another man. Not just any other man, the Boxer, cleaned up and ready to be back on top.

"Where've you been?" growled the Broker. "Not word from you in weeks."

"Well, you haven't called me either," she said. "You just went and dropped away."

She held onto her boxer even tighter.

"I haven't had a dime to take you anywhere," he snapped, doing his best to stand tall. "Things have been rough. I thought we had something going. That you'd at least come by to check on me. Just 'cause I'm down now doesn't mean I'll be like this forever. You with this guy now?"

The Boxer smiled and tried to step between the two of them. The band stopped to watch the scene unfold. I'd never heard it that quiet in St. Nick's Pub.

"No need to get in the middle of this, baby. I got it," she said, like a mother bear pushing her cub behind her. "Besides, me and him weren't much of anything anyway. I could never be with a man who lived just to live. I need someone who is after the world. Someone who wants that title to himself. Like you. Even if you don't become a champion, you still went after what you wanted." She turned to the Broker, who was slumped over on his barstool.

"What the hell did you ever go after?" she asked.

"I went after you," he responded.

"You don't know shit, boy," she said. "Don't you know it's the woman who chooses her man? A good man is usually too on his way to greatness to stop for a woman. He lets her take him. You weren't on your way anywhere, I could see that. Looks like I was right."

The Broker didn't have any responses left in him. I could tell the Boxer felt something close to empathy. I felt it too. Every man in the bar did because we've all been there, in that moment of nothing.

Not too long ago, the Boxer was begging for change, and some-how he got a second chance because the neighborhood had given it to him. That was something I was proud of.

"Baby, I saw you shadowboxing one day and I knew . . . I just knew you were my man. That sweat pouring down that beautiful body . . . mmm, yes, I knew you were mine. Just needed the comfort of the right woman was all. It's nice to have a man who needs just what a woman can give and doesn't ask for more."

The Broker was falling away piece by piece and couldn't manage the words to match hers, because none would be as true as what she had said.

The Boxer knew the feeling and bent down to whisper in the Broker's ear. I was too far away to hear and dared not move closer.

The couple walked out of St. Nick's as the band started up again.

I'd had enough. I needed my fire escape. I walked up the steps, out into the broiling night and onto the block.

I heard a match strike in the dark and turned around, trying to connect action to sound.

It was the Reporter.

"You should give me your side of everything," he said. "Just to make sure you're heard."

Damn it.

⇁

"Those pictures I got you do what you needed them to?" the Reporter asked.

"It's what the block needed," I told him. "Not me."

"Well, that money came in handy. Macon's bankroll is limitless, right?"

The way he said "right" was setting me up to correct him.

"Money didn't come from Councilman Macon," I said, keeping my pace. "We paid for that. The block."

"You want to get the word out on what you're trying to do, no?" he asked while we walked.

He had bought himself a more modern hat that fit his profession and had developed a disgusting smoking habit.

"Gives you a reason to talk to people," he said as he lit up and offered me one.

"Cancer isn't my style," I said.

He laughed, coughed, put the pack back in his shirt pocket, took out what looked like a rolled-up place mat from inside his blazer, and unrolled it, revealing it to be a computer keyboard.

He plugged it into his mobile.

"Yeah, man, this is the new breed. I don't try sending stuff into the papers anymore. I've got a blog that gets a decent amount of traffic, and that's getting me news exposure. Those old ways are dying out. Soon as this next generation has total buying power, those old institutions aren't going to have the brand recognition anymore. Dinosaurs never knew when they're going to become extinct, you know? I mean, they'll just wake up one day and they'll be gone."

His Bluetooth lit up and he looked at his phone. A picture of a woman in black leggings and beat-up Chucks came up on the screen. He smiled.

"My girl, hold on. Hey, beautiful. No. Not till late tonight. Working all night. What? Well, I'll pick up a pie before I get there. I'll let you know when I'm outside. See ya."

The little image went away and then a picture message came through, which I saw briefly. I tried to look away before he caught me but liked the fact that he did.

"Let's get down to business," he said, refocusing. "You've been calling the *Times* and asking them to run stories about what's 'going on' in the neighborhood, but you can't get them to do anything, right? You know Macon has more juice than you and he's stopping your stories. He just throwing money at them right now, but if you want to give him a real fight, you're going to need to throw something big at him. Are you prepared to sacrifice everything?"

"What the hell do you know?" I blurted out, loud enough to startle the late-night people making their way through the piles of trash on the sidewalk, looking for something to recycle.

"I know that I'm right," he shot back. "Can you say the same? I mean about how you're going about everything."

"This time I'm doing it right. The fact that I have to do it for a second time is your fault anyway."

"Let's let the past stay where it should be," he said. "You need to get around Macon. I'll start putting these stories out, but that guy is going to come after you."

"We're ready for that."

"I figured you might be."

He put the cigarette out and threw it in one of the trash cans that the kids had helped put on the block.

"See, I'm part of it," he said, tilting his head back to better hear the music coming out of the window above. "I like you, what you're doing. I want you to win. You sure about that Granderson kid, though? Where did he come from?"

"He's always been here. Most of the people on this block have always been here. Even Councilman Macon."

J Dilla blared from the lamppost on 153rd.

The chess game continued.

"See, I win no matter what," he said adjusting the brim of his hat. "I report the news. As long as the sun comes up over the Hudson each morning, I get what I need because there are always events happening. For most people, it doesn't really matter what name appears under the winner and what name goes under the loser. Most just want to know that each of those two images exist. As long as there's a good guy and a villain, people are content to read about them and believe that the world is functioning as it should. It's enough. I seek out those who are active and get with them, so that when the shit goes down, I'm there."

"So you want me to let you know when something's going down?"

"I think you doing that just might extend the lives of the people who live here. That's why," he said with finality. "I want to join up with you. I could have gone the paper route. Signed up with one of the networks or at least put myself on that path. I know how to talk to people. But I'm not about that. I'm not about giving myself to someone. I'm going to create my own, and I'd like to do that within your organization."

"We are not an organization yet," I told him.

"That's because you haven't been defined yet. That's where I come in."

We continued in silence down the block I had walked a hundred times.

CHAPTER 15

VICTORY?

1

"*Now let's play Big Bank Take Little Bank.*" —Ice Cube, "Amerikkka's Most Wanted."

The Reporter was now one of those new age journalists who didn't need the power of a network behind him to produce. He created the entire story himself. Newspapers were just starting to price themselves out of what the working classes could afford.

When I was a kid, I remember being able to buy a paper and spend hours in the back of my math class, losing myself in the box scores and replaying each game in my head just from the stats on the page. Nowadays kids were watching porn on their cell phones.

Most of the kids who came of age in the late '80s who stayed up late enough to catch Slick Rick videos on MTV at one a.m., those of us who saw *Do the Right Thing* in movie theaters, were lucky because we came along between the digital and analog ages. The last golden age in America.

That age stopped abruptly when we got a little older and saw our parents fading away in front of us. The world had changed so quickly on them that one day they woke up and found that their places on the assembly line were no longer necessary.

The outsides of those buildings we walked into tricked us into believing a life could be lived on interoffice emails. That the paychecks would keep coming in even though we were doing less, producing less, and achieving less. Even worse than that, our titles were getting more ridiculous: director of user experience, information architect, VP copy associate, and director of business development. We called ourselves royalty and sat down in chairs that destroyed the very shape of our spines and took pills to dull the pain we were causing ourselves.

I was no longer a part of any of that, but I couldn't erase what I had learned. I had thought that because I had become part of a righteous fight, I might achieve a true sense of nobility.

The Reporter figured that the best human interest story was Sukal, so we used her as the launch for the publicity campaign that would draw Councilman Macon into the light.

He recorded Sukal packing up her boxes and deciding what memories to throw away, editing in images of her valuables being picked through on the streets. He included scenes of others who had been forced to move. After he put it out on the Web, it went viral within days.

Soon, people started to arrive on the block with picket signs, joining the ones we had planted there to get it started. The gathering got bigger. Finally, the networks arrived, because even though they were on Councilman Macon's payroll, he couldn't match ad revenue. Being the one station that missed out on a big story always hurts the ratings. News teams have to be perceived as the honest voice. They work hard at keeping that image alive.

2

I woke in late afternoon to the sounds of trucks, helicopter blades, and police sirens. Namuna was on her third cup of coffee and finishing up a floor plan next to me.

"What the hell is that?" I said.

"Macon has outdone himself," she replied. "I must say, the execution of this plan seems flawless, which means it's time you should be making contingencies. Perhaps that's what your friend is doing, smoking on our fire escape."

"Can't stop motion," I said, taking the coffee out of her hands and sipping myself awake.

Namuna smiled at the intimacy of the moment but didn't say anything.

The Reporter was sitting outside, performing his own morning ritual: filming, writing, taking pictures, and talking into his earpiece.

"Welcome to the day," he said. "Man, looks like you're getting at least a little of what you wanted."

"What do you mean?"

He pointed to the window next to me, and I looked inside to see Sukal sitting there with Councilman Macon, smiling and praising him.

"This man gave me back my place," she said to the cameraman, before turning back to Councilman Macon. "I owe everything to you, Councilman."

"My dear, as long as I am running the show around here, I assure you that these buildings will be full of the people who rightfully belong inside of them. It is for that reason that, in fact, we have just purchased this apartment for you. Now it will be yours until your last days. And by the looks of you, that won't be for quite some time."

They all laughed. Councilman Macon noticed me watching through the window. The cameras stopped rolling. His mood changed, but nobody noticed except me. Maybe I knew his behaviors so well because they mirrored much of what I kept hidden. He shook hands until the cameramen and reporters made their way out the door. Sukal was tired and needed to take a seat.

"Would you mind if I stepped out to your fire escape?" Councilman Macon asked. "I haven't been on one of these since I was a child. I grew up around here you know."

"I do know and I don't mind. This has all been so much for me. I just want to sit for a spell. You do what you need to out there."

He came out and sat next to us as if we had invited him. His first words were directed at the Reporter.

"You did a hell of a job getting this old woman back in here. Played it just right."

"Just played it how it needed to be played is all," the Reporter said.

"I could use a man like you in my operation," Councilman Macon said in the same tone he'd used when he first approached me.

"I'm sure you could, but I have my own operation and I'm doing just fine. Thanks, though."

The Reporter reached for a cigarette only to find his pack empty. Councilman Macon was at the ready with a silver case.

"It's a stressful job being me," he said, then took one for himself and lit it. He moved to light the one that the Reporter had taken but was brushed away.

"I got it," replied the Reporter, lighting his own cigarette and leaning back on the bricks with the satisfaction of having delivered a line he'd been looking to deliver to a man like Councilman Macon for a long, long time.

There was a moment of silence before Councilman Macon turned his attention to me.

"You think you're going to come out victorious, but that is impossible. You can't go any further without some help. We own everything from 155th down to 145th. Ask your friend there. He knows. He has all the records."

"It's true," the Reporter said. "He does. But he can't move on anything now. It's too hot."

"This is true," Councilman Macon laughed, enjoying the challenge. "However, time moves on, and this swell of attention will pass. That woman next door will die. When she does or how she does, it's of no matter. And who holds her apartment? Who holds the building?"

"We'll keep fighting you," I said, starting to lose my cool.

"You think you've seen what we can do? This is only the start. I have people on the streets now working against you. That man makes a fine trumpet player for sure, but he has a family and a grandmother just about the same age as this woman right here. We have just purchased her apartment for her as well. I think that'll cause him to back off for a while. What do you think about that?"

I looked over at the Reporter as he finished his cigarette.

Councilman Macon looked me straight in the eyes.

"Do you honestly believe anyone cares more about your movement than about their family? My son, you have a great deal of heart but not too much of anything else. I'm just a little jealous of how pure you want to be—not how pure you are, mind you—but what you are attempting. Don't fool yourself into thinking people are not going to take the best deal for themselves and their people. That's politics."

"I'm not interested in politics," I told him.

"What interests you has no bearing on the world around you."

The words hit me like a Tyson uppercut, but I stayed focused.

"I'm going to fight that concept until I can't move," I said.

"Do you have the stomach to go further?" he asked. "How much can you stand to lose? How about that woman in the bedroom? You think you would feel the same without her? I'm just saying, I'm where I am because I didn't let things like right and wrong decide my fate and the fate of my family. I'm the kind of man who knows what he believes. I have no problem doing what I need to do to protect what I have. You'll never see me sweeping up a street, unless a camera is pointed at me, of course. Bad things can happen very easily. Don't count on the public to change too much. Now, if you want to deal with me, that's another question altogether. I will give you this victory, but the game . . . the game is always mine."

"So what is it you want?" I asked. "If what you say is true, you don't need me for anything anymore. You said you're just going to wait us out. Go on and wait, then. I'm not giving up, and if you even think about doing anything to my wife, I'll hang you in the middle of the street and let the neighborhood take everything out on you."

"That may happen, though I doubt it," he replied calmly. "You are not the revenge type. I think that violence is too real for you. To resort to it would be the end of you. A war is something you cannot win. You have been fighting well enough to walk away proud."

I turned to the Reporter, looking for a sign from him.

"Can I win?" I asked.

"Anybody can win," he replied.

Councilman Macon climbed down the fire escape all the way to the street.

"I couldn't trust him again," I said to the Reporter. "Not after last time."

"Thing is," he said, "trust has nothing to do with it. You shouldn't trust anyone, not even me. I mean, I believe in you, I'm down for your cause, but who knows what turns my life is going to take. Twenty years from now I could be in a very different place. We might not know each other then. But for now I'm with you. I have enough information on Macon to get him good, but he knows that, and I have a bad feeling he's going to try and get rid of me. So I'm going away for a bit. My profile is too high to stick around. I'll have to operate from a different place."

"Who's going to bring the truth out now?" I asked.

"My part is done," he said. "Make sure you walk away with yourself intact before this is all over. Don't make the mistake of thinking it won't end. Everything does."

He too crawled down the fire escape and headed up the block. He made a right just before the bridge and disappeared.

Namuna came out with a few beers and we sat together. The last of the fireworks—the ones that hadn't been set off on the Fourth—ignited from the rooftops. The Bodega Guy had stocked up on a bunch from Chinatown and continued to hand them out to all the kids in the neighborhood.

One by one, each of the rooftops exploded their fireworks into the sky above.

The sky lit up in purple and orange, blue and red, and a white that blended with the night stars. Everyone stopped for a moment. Fireworks do that, perhaps because they allow you to look up into the sky without having to think of the earth below.

3

When the Bodega Guy sat on his windowsill, with his feet up on a cooler and holding the remote control to the stereo plugged into the lamppost, people would stop as they walked by to pay their respects. He was running some operation. Every once in a while, a car would pull up and double-park. The driver would get out and leave the car there, or pop the hood open and pretend to be fixing some mechanical problem. Five minutes later, the Bodega Guy would walk slowly to the car, ease himself in, sit inside for about thirty seconds, then walk back out to his window. Thirty seconds after that, someone would come over, take a package from him, hop into a car of his own, drive off somewhere, and come back on foot.

The music would start up again and stay on until all hours of the night. He didn't care. Even when the block was empty, he would stand there, his hat tilted to the side, blasting music and dancing around by himself. Once in a while there would be a shout to turn the music down but he never did, except to talk to one of the people holding up the wall.

Most of the time the shouts came from me. Namuna always told me it was my shouting that would wake everyone up, not the music.

From above, he looked like the villain.

One by one the kids ran through the fire hydrant. The older girls hung back, and the boys kept looking over their shoulders at the girls, who were all now developing and of much more interest than the water shooting out of a hydrant.

The old folks sat back and watched it all, having seen the cycle many times before.

"How could I leave any of this?" Namuna said. "There's just no place in the world like it."

"Without you up here," I said, "none of this would be worth watching."

We leaned in to kiss, but the blasting bass from a car that had pulled up in front of the Bodega made it hard to hear our hearts pound.

I'd had enough.

I charged downstairs and crossed the street, flexing myself and puffing out as hard as I could. The spray from the fire hydrant fell but did nothing to cool me off. Now getting a closer look at the man, I noticed just how far his belly stuck out and how absurd he looked holding his cigarette between his pudgy fingers.

"Why the hell do you have to blast that for the whole neighborhood to hear? Nobody wants to listen to that!"

The Bodega Guy and his crew just started laughing. At their feet were empty packs of smokes and the containers from their dinners. They were standing in their own filth. I could feel the eyes of the people watching from the windows around us. They didn't care either way about the outcome, they just wanted a little drama in their evenings. Nothing on TV was ever as good as what went down on the street.

His face was harder up close, without so much as a drop of fear in it. I looked back up and saw Namuna watching from the fire escape. She hadn't wanted me to come down.

"Who the fuck are you?" he asked, looking back at his friends to make sure they'd stepped up with him.

"I live across the street. Just trying to have an evening of peace and quiet with my wife. We've talked about this before."

"My music is the music of this block, eh. We've been listening to this music long before you got here. Maybe you need to adjust?"

"I'm here now, and I told you to turn it down. And while I'm here, why not pick up some of this shit on the ground? We've almost got this block clean, and here you are trashing everything. Have a little respect."

"You telling me about respect?" he laughed. "You come down here and call me out in front of my people? Fuck that. Fuck you. You best go back upstairs and chill the fuck out before I shut you up like we use to do."

He turned the music even louder. Everyone was hanging out their windows at this point. A kid came up carrying two black, wrinkled plastic bags and nodded at the Bodega Guy. The Bodega Guy nodded back to the boy and sneered at me, leaving the conversation because he had no need to continue.

He followed the skinny kid holding the bags inside, and I walked slowly back across the street. The windows slid back down all around me. The gypsy cabs pulled up and away, and the flow of the bloodstream continued. In front of our building, more U-Haul trucks sat parked. We stopped what we could, but it was impossible to fend off everyone.

"What you need to do is concentrate that energy on something else."

The voice came from Crossing Guard Lita.

"Yeah, I'm talking to you," she continued, after telling her dogs to pipe down. "I saw what you tried to do there. That took some balls."

I leaned up against the wall underneath her window. A man sporting tight cornrows came out of the Bodega, jumped on his motorcycle, revved it a few times, and took off down the block. You could hear the car alarms going off as he roared by, setting each of them off with his vibrations.

"What are you after?" she said, pulling on a joint. "That's for medical reasons, son. You want some?"

I took a drag, and the weight lifted off my shoulders right away. It had been a few years since I had gotten high, and the wait made everything even more delightful. After blowing the smoke out, I felt as if it was the first time I had exhaled in a long, long while.

"Well, give it back to me, son. Ms. Lita needs her some to keep the pain from coming back."

I reached up and handed it back to her, and she casually smoked it like a cigarette. The music didn't seem so loud now. The hydrant was even more beautiful than before. One of the older boys—a tall muscle-bound kid, his physique visible even through his XXL white T-shirt and droopy jeans separated from the sidewalk by a pair of Timberlands, had gotten the attention of one of the girls. His head was bent down low so that only she could hear his whispers, but her friend, a little younger, sat inches away on the steps, pretending to look away, trying her hardest to listen. Some dude a few feet from them was checking her out, but she had no intention of doing anything about it. Caught between playing in the hydrant and emulating the couple who were now making their way up the block, she decided to just sit there and wait.

"Ain't nothing ever clean," Lita continued. "The world just doesn't work like that. When you like these kids over here, maybe you can think that it's going to be perfect. But you and I both know that it ain't. Nature's not wired that way. You live. You die. You feel pain. You play. You experience loss. And when your back's up against it, you fight just to survive or for what you want to survive. Those who don't do that . . ."

She trailed off and gazed over at those who had stopped making choices and stayed on the block, only traveling back and forth between subway stops.

"Don't get me wrong about any of that. I still love everyone. Seen them grow from pups, you know? You too. I remember when you all pulled in here in that beat-up van with California plates. You were looking around like you were in the Twilight Zone or something. Now look at you. You're trying to find a way to keep it like it is. Like it was. Like you thought it was."

"I liked it like that," I told her.

"I'll tell you this," she said through a slight cough and with a tone of resignation, "things are never going to be like they were. That's why the sun comes up new every day. Make your choices and know that you're going to have to give something away."

She nodded at me but didn't smile.

I knew if I could get the Bodega Guy out of the picture, I'd be able to make the block how I felt it needed to be. Only problem was that, while Granderson had control of the streets, it was the Bodega Guy who ran the underground. No amount of tax revenue was going to force his hand.

"Macon," I said to myself.

I reached into my pocket and pulled out his business card. I already knew the number by heart, but I needed something tangible to help me consider what I was about to do. I looked up and saw that Namuna had left the fire escape, the candles had nearly burned down, and the only movement was the curtain blowing in the slight breeze.

I knew what I had to do, which had little to do with what I wanted.

In the end, it never looks how you think it will.

4

The third meeting with Councilman Macon was at a Dunkin' Donuts, a new one, that had just been constructed above the subway stop on 145th Street. The place had been an old jazz lounge for a long time, then an abandoned storefront for longer than that, and had managed to keep the old sign hanging out in front.

"Quite an establishment," Councilman Macon said, stirring his chocolate drink. "Folks here should like having this as a choice beside that Starbucks down the block, don't you think?"

"I would have liked to see the family-owned shop up in 147th stand alone around here, if you ask me."

"Well, I didn't ask you. Had I done that, we'd be sitting in an abandoned club at this moment, wouldn't we?"

"Should have just built the club back up," I said.

"People don't want to see that when they're looking for new areas to live. They want to see familiar signs—items that are recognizable."

"Brands."

"Exactly. Yes, that's right, you used to work in advertising. What ever happened there?"

"I woke up with a conscience one morning."

"That should not have prevented you from doing what you enjoyed doing. It never did for me."

"Well, I'm not like you," I said.

"Don't be so quick to assess that as a fact."

We both paused there for a moment, sizing each other up and wondering how many of our cards we were going to have to show. He was ready to deal. He had everything in place, even the big money. He just wanted my little war to end.

"I want to keep my block," I said to him.

"Your block," he laughed. "And what is it you're looking to keep?"

"I want the people there to stay there. Take what you want below 145th, but that last block, until 155th, that's mine."

He sat back and thought about something he hadn't considered before.

"And then you'll call off the attacks?" he asked. "You'll keep that reporter off my back?"

"The attacks I can do something about. You have my word they won't spread below 145th. The Reporter has always worked on his own. I can't stop him from doing what he's doing. Freedom of the press, you know."

"I'll deal with him in my own way, then," Councilman Macon said. "I assume you still want the police protection around your area. The drugs and all that? I would venture to guess that's a little too authentic for you. You still need my people to help with that?"

"Just keep this damn place as clean as you can, and if I see those trucks going up past 145th, things are going to blow up. Understand?"

"Understood. Is that everything?"

"No, it's not. There's one other problem. The dude who owns the Bodega, he's got to go. Can you take care of that?" After I said it, I felt a sense of regret but could not fully understand it.

"With one phone call I could, but you had better think carefully about what you're asking. I know the man you're talking about. He may seem bad to you, but you never know what's going to take his place. The devil you know . . . well, you know the rest of the expression."

"Let me worry about what comes next, you just take care of what comes now."

I extended my hand to shake his, completed the transaction, and headed out.

I walked back up the block, trying forget everything below 145th Street.

I thought that somehow this was going to make my block safe, but when you start thinking that a city block is yours, you are blinding yourself to reality.

5

I was inside when the lights from the sirens flashed through the apartment. The sounds followed. I opened the window, a sound that joined the chorus of windows opening all around me.

The Bodega Guy was being taken out in handcuffs. He wasn't so tough looking anymore. The police took off his hat so the entire neighborhood could see just who this guy was. I thought I would derive some kind of pleasure from watching all of this, from seeing him being hauled off, but there was a feeling in my gut that told me the wrong man was being taken away. My phone rang.

"That's what you wanted, right?" the voice said.

I looked around, expecting to see him sitting in a giant director's chair drinking Metaxa Grande Fine Greek Brandy and smoking a cigarillo. But no. He wasn't there. Not at all. Why would he be? He was the person making it all happen, so there was no need to be close to the action. The only one watching who had any knowledge of what was really happening was me.

As they put the Bodega Guy in the police car, a stream of children followed after him. These were the same kids who hung out on his wall and played under the fire hydrants that he'd helped unlock in front of the building. They screamed with dry throats.

Slowly, bottles and whatever else people could spare started flying out of the windows and shattering on the street. They almost drowned out the shouts. I could see that the Bodega Guy was scanning the crowd, looking to see who had done this to him.

The car pulled away, and the block was silent. The people hanging out of the windows, after looking around to make sure the action had ended, shut them and went back inside. The men standing in front of the Bodega closed it up slowly and drank a final beer together before tossing the cans on the street and walking away.

I tried to sleep, but I found that I couldn't without the sounds I had grown accustomed to. The silence made my thoughts sound more like screams of anguish than subtle murmurings. I stayed up long into the hot night, without a word from the street or a hint of breeze whistling through caverns formed by the buildings.

"This is what you wanted," said Namuna, taking off her glasses and rolling over to sleep.

Is this what you wanted?

The night was eerier now, and figures weaved through the lampposts. I wished the ghosts from the block would come visit me, but they lay dormant, asleep in their graves.

I envied them.

Kissing Namuna lightly so that I wouldn't disturb her, I went out for a walk up to 155th and found my friend sitting by the Macombs Dam Bridge, waiting for the sun to come up.

"Mind if I wait with you?" I asked.

"You don't have too much time to just sit around anymore. Things are going to start changing quick round here. With him gone, things are gonna blow up. Plus, all those people coming from midtown, man, this situation is no good."

"Nobody is going to touch this block anymore," I told him. "This block here is mine. I'll take care of things."

"Oh, you going to be the man now, huh? You gonna take care of people like that Bodega Guy did? Shoot, he had his hand in everything, had this block on lock 24/7. That man was righteous. Can't believe somebody did him like that."

"Power shifts," I told him. "You have to realize that."

"Man, power up here, in these streets, needs to be stable. Shifting is no good. Why does everyone want to change a world that already works? I think some folks are just bored or scared of their own lives so they go about changing the world around them instead of themselves. What do you think about that?"

"I think the world around us is an extension of ourselves. If we let it get out of control, we'll never be able to take care of anyone."

"You have no control over the world around you. You can try, but somebody is always, and I mean always, going to come around and undo what you went and did. Bet that."

I looked out over the Harlem River, where they were just putting the final touches on the new Yankee Stadium.

"Funny," the Kid said.

"What's funny?"

"They did some renovations a couple years back. They wanted to make it all modern-looking, wanted it to compete with the new ballparks being built around the country like Busch and Shea. Now they're building a new stadium and making it look all retro so it feels like the original Yankee Stadium. If they had just left the first one alone, they wouldn't have had to change a thing. I'm about leaving shit alone."

The stars lined up like a road in the dark sky. He started to walk toward the stadium.

"Where you going?" I asked.

"Got a ticket for the game today. Found it on the subway yesterday. Can't wait."

He turned and looked up at the building on the corner of Edgecomb Avenue. "I never really noticed it before," he said, "but that building curves around the block."

He walked backward across the bridge toward Yankee Stadium, watching Harlem getting smaller but bigger in his mind. I couldn't tell if he was keeping an eye on me or Harlem.

CHAPTER 16

A NEW DAY IN HARLEM

1

I woke up late the day after they took the Bodega Guy away and slow rolled out of bed down to the Chicken and Pizza Shop for a cup of coffee.

The sound of the ambulance pulling up to our apartment building faded in seamlessly to the morning activity, and it wasn't until I saw them loading in a body that I realized somebody had died.

"Sukal," said Crossing Guard Lita, cleaning up after her dogs. "She finally went. She and I been living here so long I feel like part of me is under that sheet with her."

I wanted very much to go and say something to the woman under the sheet, but there were no words. I felt at peace with the time I had spent with her while she was alive. I guess some part of me was happy that she would now be with her husband.

Namuna walked through the vestibule door just after they pulled away.

"Got to go to work," she said, breaking away from the kiss but staying close enough to whisper to me. Crossing Guard Lita sighed at the display of affection. I felt other eyes on us as well.

There was no music, only the sound of the ambulance rolling away.

"I won't be home too late," Namuna said. "The place I'm working on is right around here actually. Just below 145th."

"You're going down to 145th?" I asked, pulling back. "By all that new construction? What are you trying to do to me?"

"What am I doing to *you*? I'm not doing anything but my job, besides you told Macon you didn't care what happened below 145th. Don't be such a child. Wish me a good day, and I'll see you later."

She smiled at me and rubbed my cheek.

"You can't go down there," I said. "Especially today, what with Sukal passing. It's disrespectful."

Her smile faded.

"You want to say that again, because I couldn't hear you over the words 'who the fuck does he think he is?' running though my mind."

"That's Councilman Macon's district," I pleaded. "You're putting money in his pocket."

"I'm putting money in our pockets as well. Don't forget that, and don't judge me. I let you be you, don't I? Start living for the living already."

I wouldn't let go.

"You're taking away my manhood. My own wife selling out the soul of the neighborhood."

"I think you're the one who sold the soul of this neighborhood," she snapped. "Why don't you look around at what you did? I'd like to look with you, but I have to go to work. One of us has to."

She took off. I could have gone after her. I should have.

2

The sounds of building construction from below 145th rumbled up our way as I walked by the Chess-Playing Kids.

"Thanks, man," the older one said. "Just wanted to let you know it's much appreciated what you did. My auntie was saying prayers for you all night. You good people in our book."

"Thanks," I answered. "Never really sure what I'm doing is the right thing."

"I didn't say all that now," he said, looking over his pawns. "I just said thanks. Right or wrong is up to a higher power, you know?"

"I thought you said your aunt was praying for me," I said. "Sounds like she's happy."

Throughout the conversation, he never took his eyes off the board.

"She's old-school, though," he said, almost making a move, then changing his mind. "Really old-school. She still remembers when jazz clubs and that kind of stuff ruled this block. It's a different time now though, man. No suits running these streets. Matter of fact, after last night, nothing running these streets. We might be moving this game inside the vestibule for a bit. You don't know what could be going down round here now that the block is no longer on lockdown, you know?"

"You mean the dudes from the Bodega not being here, right?" I said, trying to sound like I had no idea what he was talking about.

"Yep, yep."

"Damn it," the younger one said, leaning back to see if changing her perspective would change the situation of the game. It didn't.

3

When a building collapses, it's not just the sound of the bricks making the noise. Ghosts who have lived inside the walls, who have left life in the building's fabric because they were not allowed to take to it the other side, cry out as the last attachment to their losses is finally destroyed.

The dust rose quickly over the block.

A few of the neighborhood kids, led by the Green Fitted Hat Kid, ran up the street. They were covered in what looked to be ash and kept twisting their necks to look behind them.

"What the hell are you all running from?" I yelled.

"We're just doing some final touches, you know. We're taking back the neighborhood. Like you said to do. Come on, man. Don't act all surprised. We thought you'd like this one. Nobody is going to be moving into that building for a while now."

They gave each other dap.

"You did this? We made a deal with Councilman Macon. Do you know what he'll do if he finds out?"

Granderson came up from the rear and tried to pass by without saying a word.

"He gave us this block," I told him "We can build from here. I don't understand the purpose of destroying buildings. What made you do it?"

"Nothing made me do it," he said, waving the little ones on and stepping up to my face. "Besides, you should know that nobody can give or take a block. You wrote that, right?"

"What about the people inside that building? How many must have died? My God!"

"I've seen enough of that in my lifetime that I can't lose more sleep over it than I already do. I'm safe, you're safe, and our families are safe. Everyone else we're at war with."

"That wasn't the plan."

"Fuck the plan," he said. "We needed a little more room. With the money we're generating with our tax revenues, plus the projections of what our block-owned businesses are going to start pulling in, we're going to have to plan for expansion."

He saw the confused look on my face and waved at the others to go on without him.

"We didn't hurt anyone. They were going to show apartments later today. They already cleared everyone out. Those folks have been displaced now, right? So we showed them what happens when you displace people, right? Right!"

The kids went on their way, led by Granderson, past our block and up into Washington Heights. Some of them vanished down the hill that used to be the Polo Grounds. I stood still on the block. The sound of a plane above was the only noise—one that highlighted how quiet everything was.

After the thrill of something breaking up the monotony of their day, people started walking down the block, getting back to their usual motions. I enjoyed watching the trees being planted, the garbage being swept away, the fruit carts from local farmers being set up and the anti-smoking murals being painted on what used to be the training building for the fire department.

This was the satisfaction I had been looking for, and I let it override the fact that a few people had gone rogue and started enacting their own plans. That is life, I thought. That is indeed the will of the people.

I waited on the block for Namuna to come back. I was sure she knew more about what happened and could tell me if anyone was hurt. Usually I could tell it was her coming. I could see her face from two blocks away. Her smile. Her cheeks. The way she moved.

A hand on my shoulder. It was the Reporter with an empty look on his face. The eager young man who had always just been after a story now looked like he had seen too much. The youth was gone from him.

His hand shook as he tried to keep a grip on his camera.

"You were there," I asked. "You got it?"

He said nothing.

"That's the footage of a lifetime if you did. You'll be able to get the entire city behind us. We could ask for more from Councilman Macon now. Hell, we could get him to do repairs to the buildings *and* keep the people living there. This might not have been the worst thing after all. He'll have to take responsibility for it."

I was starting to get excited again. Those kids were right. The movement didn't have to stop just because a deal had been made. The neighborhood was starting to take care of itself. That was my thought. My spirits lifted just then. Can you believe that?

THE LAST BLOCK IN HARLEM   199

"You don't know. You don't know yet."

"Know what?" I asked.

"Namuna . . ."

He couldn't say it, but he didn't have to. I put it together from there. She had been on-site to check out the apartments as people were moving in. She was making her business around there so she could be near me instead of going overseas. She did it for me.

I saw in the eyes of the Reporter a man looking at a man who just lost his wife. I wanted to run toward the rubble and cut myself on the rocks so I could join her. That was my first thought, but my body wouldn't move. Excuse me, please, even writing this now, it is a struggle to remember that moment, the moment I lost her. I'm trying these days to put it out of me, but I've never—I can't.

The day faded away.

4

I couldn't go back inside the apartment after the funeral. I buried her up in the Trinity Church graveyard so she could be close to me, though I was unsure of why I was doing it. There was no reason to keep her close to me. I didn't believe in mourning the dead.

This time it was the silence that kept me up, so what I did was stay out on the block and pass out in some random spot. Everything was clean by then, and I was the blemish. Granderson made sure that wherever I passed out, someone would put me back into my vestibule.

On it went like that for months. Addiction happens fast when you're looking for it. My face was starting to tan too much—I was exposed to a sun that never seemed to fade. That summer never went away. I wandered up and down the block, no doubt becoming a character in some writer's story, looking for some reality to create from. The people who I'd helped averted their eyes when I stumbled by. They fed me, though. Gave me water. Gave me a safe place to pass out. Up here, people understood that sometimes folks just fall down.

If I were downtown I would have been stepped over, but the block, the people here, took me in as their own once they saw how far I had dropped away.

They'd used the taxes to help with a magnificent funeral. The Preacher said words he believed would deliver her to God. Why would God take my wife away from me in the first place? All of that went by fast though. Sukal was right. After it all ends, all you are is alone. I didn't mind being the drunk. I was living off of the block and that suited me fine.

At the graveyard fence, I drank as much as I could and called out to Namuna's fresh grave but never heard anything back.

"You need to stop screaming out to her and accept the fact that she's gone," said Crossing Guard Lita, coming down the street pushing a cart filled with soil and a few shovels.

"I'm not ready to do that," I said. "I don't think I'll ever be ready to do that."

"Why don't you take a walk with me up to the community garden," she said. "It might do you good to work the land a little bit. Might keep you away from yourself. Sometimes a man just needs to get out of his own way."

We walked a bit down St. Nicholas Place, then made a right onto 153rd and walked up the incline until we reached a garden. Not lush, but you could tell that it was heading that way. A few kids helped till the soil while the older folks sat on the benches, telling them what to do.

"Here, take this," she said, handing me a shovel. "Why don't you go and move that dirt out of the way so these children can get to planting. Work this garden as long as you can, and then be on your way. Just know that it's always here and never locked, so when you need to work that mind and keep it from drifting, you can come up here."

"Did we build this with tax revenues?" I asked.

"My father started this garden twenty-five years ago. I've been coming here since it opened to keep his legacy going."

"I never noticed it before."

"Sometimes it helps to get off your block."

She smiled, and I started to dig up dirt, using my muscles for the first time in months. The only thing I had carried from one piece of concrete to the next was my body, and I hadn't even been doing that great a job of that. Days, maybe weeks, passed this way. The meaning of time that had at one point driven me to fight so hard had dissolved.

I could usually hold my concentration for about an hour before I needed a drink. One day I went back to the Bodega to get a brew and there he was, hat tilted, dancing to his music in front of his spot.

The Bodega Guy had gotten out.

5

"When did you get out?" I asked.

"I'm not really out," he said, rolling up his pant leg and exposing one of those house arrest bracelets, which looked to be carving a pretty hefty groove into the bottom of his leg. "They didn't have room for me there, so they decided to make me a prisoner in my home. Fucking technology, eh?"

"I've never seen you opening up the Bodega before," I said.

"I'm not opening anything, just getting some hot sauce for my breakfast."

He looked at me, knowing what happened to me but passing on saying anything about it.

"Funny that you're down here with me," he said, turning on his radio. "Well, maybe not so funny. You hungry?"

He didn't wait for me to answer before he yelled for his wife to fix another plate, which she did, and put it on the windowsill next to his.

"Come on," he said. "Let's eat."

"Thanks," I said. "Usually get a sandwich or something up at the garden, then come down here for something to drink."

After I said it, I remembered all of the times I would look down at them from my apartment and shake my head at the fact that they were drinking in the middle of the day. Now there weren't many times when I wasn't drinking, unless I had a shovel in my hand moving dirt from one place to another.

Crossing Guard Lita would hang out of her window and tell me I wasn't spending enough time in the garden. I thought I was giving her plenty, but I figured she just wanted to keep an eye on me and keep me rooted in reality as much as she could.

I sat down to eat breakfast with the Bodega Guy, and we both took in St. Nicholas Place from his side of the block. I kept my eyes on the concrete to avoid having to look up to our apartment. I couldn't help thinking of it as anything but ours.

"You're not running the Bodega anymore?" I asked.

"Nah, no more ownership for me. Condition of the release. Made me sign it away."

"I'm sure you have someone else running it in name only," I said, pouring as much hot sauce as I could stand on the eggs. "After all, the person the public sees is never the one who's really running the show."

"Not here, man," he said, jerking his head back and looking at me from under the brim of his hat. "Here, you need to be in front of what you own."

"I never thought of it like that."

"That's because you're not from here."

"That's true," I answered. "Not sure where I'm going either. Not sure I can stay here after what happened, but how am I supposed to decide where to go? Right now, this block is all I have."

"Welcome to what I've woken up to my whole life," he said, taking the last scoop of his food and tossing his plate into the gutter.

He stopped me from speaking anymore until he had unlocked the ice machine and pulled out a small radio. He whistled once, and a little kid who had been sitting on the stoop just a few buildings down took the stereo to the bottom of the lamppost, plugged it in, and turned it up.

"Now we can speak freely without worrying about being heard, right?"

One of the great mysteries of my world was revealed just like that, as he lit up a smoke and rubbed his belly.

"Why do you smoke?" I asked. "I mean, you're older now. I smoked when I was young because it was cool and they got me a little buzzed, but I stopped when I no longer knew the top ten of the top forty. What keeps you going? Do you like it?"

"I don't do things because I like to do them. I do them because they are part of who I am. I've been smoking since the day I got out here. My dad smoked, the guys before who owned this spot smoked, I smoke. I don't have time to stop what I do. Don't judge me on it."

"Just saying that you'll live longer and maybe the kid who takes over this place after you will see something different. You know, you could stop the cycle."

He smiled.

"For someone who wants to keep things as they are, you sure are stuck on wanting everyone around you to change. Just got to let things take their course. Like our good councilman. Never see those posters around here anymore, do you?"

"No, I suppose you don't," I said.

"Let me tell you," he said. "A man has to hold himself up to his entire life without any do-overs, you know what I mean, eh? You have to take all of it in. Without standing up for such things, you're not a man. All your mistakes, all your scars, everything you've done wrong, that's what makes us who we are."

He took his final drag from his smoke and was about to flick it into the street when he stopped short. He put it out inside an empty beer can and smiled at me.

"That make you happy?" he asked

"It would if you recycled the can," I said, almost smiling.

6

I got more and more comfortable hanging out on that side of the street with the guys at the Bodega. They gave me free beer, and we would talk late into the night. Although I didn't understand the songs that were coming out of the radio, I still danced in hopes of shaking my demons loose.

One night, through the blurred eyes of too many Coors Lights, I saw a U-Haul truck pull up. A young couple, moving cautiously from the doors while they checked out their surroundings, started to move their furniture from the street into the building. He told her to wait by the van while he moved all of their things up the stairs. After a few trips, she became anxious and tried to lift the TV off the back herself but stumbled badly. Driven by instinct, I rushed across the street to help her and caught it just before it hit the ground.

"Thank you, sir," she said. "I just don't know what I was thinking."

"Well, welcome to the neighborhood anyway," I said, not wanting to initiate a conversation or connection.

The man, who must have been her husband (I could tell by the way he charged out to the street to see who this other man was with his wife), picked up the TV, moved it to safety, and came back to the scene in what seemed like one fluid motion.

"Everything fine here?" he said, stroking her hair and looking at me with some curiosity.

"Yes, this man helped save our TV!" she said. "What was your name again?"

"What apartment are you moving into?" I asked.

"Forty-three," he said.

"Then I'm your neighbor," I told them. "Though I guess I haven't spent too much time in my place over the past few months. No."

With that, I kind of shuffled away, back to the Bodega to continue getting my drunk on. For me, that's all there was. I stayed away from St. Nick's and most every place other than the Bodega. They had kept calling me sir, which I understood when, in the reflection of the ice cooler, I noticed my hair getting gray.

The Reporter walked up behind me, causing my reflection to look even more out of focus.

"Macon is going to take the mayor's office soon if we don't stop him," he said.

"I think you may have mistaken me for someone else," I said. "Or perhaps your memory is not what it should be."

"He bled you dry and is using your work to continue his legacy."

"Let him do it," I stammered. "That'll be my ultimate revenge. Seeing him live out the same fate as me. Legacy indeed!"

I finished my beer and reached into the ice machine to grab another.

"You're a disgrace," he said, making no attempts to stop me. "You should have just stayed a nobody behind a desk. At least you would have died without a witness."

He left pissed off but came back a few days later to try to rile me up to join his crusade, but it wasn't in me. The only reason I returned to the apartment was to feed Knight and clean up his litter. That much I had left in me to do. I never went farther than the kitchen. After I fed him, I'd sit for a bit and then leave, feeling such pressure from the emptiness of the house.

He kept waiting for Namuna to come home and sat by the door around the time she would normally walk through it. With the passing days, he started to realize that she was not coming back.

I would allow myself a brief memory of how she would sit there for hours at her desk, focused on her task, or how she would move carefully in the morning before she let her feet touch the floor. Then those memories would fade out, and I would be left again in the empty space and the certainty of time alone. Had it not been for Knight, I probably would have killed myself.

The more I hung out in front of the Bodega, the more I depleted whatever savings I had until I was pretty much broke. The Reporter stopped coming around. The block itself was doing well. Councilman Macon stayed true to his word and did not go farther with the gentrification of the neighborhood than 145th Street, but all around us Harlem was changing. I didn't care.

The summer passed without me noticing, and the changing leaves that I had always looked forward to did nothing for me. I raked them away at the garden because Crossing Guard Lita kept bugging me to spend time there, but it didn't do anything for me. I still stopped by the graveyard on the way there and back, and sobbed looking through the fence.

Thing about the weather turning colder is that you need to eat more, and with my money dwindling, my ability to buy food became nonexistent. I needed work. Real work. Money work.

I went to the library up on 160th and used their computer to put together a résumé. I contacted a few of the recruiters who had found me work in the past, and before I left the library that day, I had scored an interview for a senior copywriter position at an interactive agency in midtown. These jobs are not too difficult to get if you have the résumé for such things.

I can remember being in the lobby of the giant building and looking into the mirror, trying to make myself appear younger and stop sweating. I could do neither. I wasn't sweating because I was nervous, but because I was afraid for the life I was entering back into.

By the time I walked into the reception area of the office, I felt as if I had moved back in time. It was pretty much like every other place I had ever worked for. A woman bursting with personality for those worth bursting for sat answering phones and saying hello back to whoever walked past her. She didn't ask me who I was there to see, forcing me to approach her, at which point she shot me a dirty look and told me to sit down. I would have liked a glass of water.

About twenty-five minutes later, a man came out wearing jeans, a black T-shirt, and a smile. He extended his hand and led me into his office. The walls were bare, and he looked at his computer screen more than he did at me.

"Did you bring a copy of your résumé?" he asked, looking through a stack of papers, trying to find mine. "I had it here somewhere . . . yes, here it is. I see it's been a while since you worked full-time. What have you been doing with yourself?"

"I took some time off," I told him, pausing, but not getting lost in reflection. "Personal reasons."

"I hear ya. Before I came aboard here, I spent a month in Madagascar playing with those ring-tailed lemurs," he said, stopping himself from laughing. "Would have stayed longer but there was a coup or something. Anyway, looks like you were working on some interesting stuff before your time off. We do mostly interactive cross-media promotions here. We need someone who can work with the team but stay independent, stay out of the box but not ignore it, got it? The brands we represent are very much committed to staying on message. Did you bring your book?"

I handed him my portfolio, and he started flipping through it, making sure that the work in there wasn't any better than he could do.

"This seems good," he said closing it up and handing it back to me. "Do you have any questions for me?"

Now it had been a while since I was on an interview, but I remembered that this was the biggest question asked. Here they just wanted to see what kind of person you were and if they would be able to handle you on a day-to-day basis. In my mind, I played out the next year of my life in there. I saw all the people looking into the office and trying not to look at the same time. New blood usually means that they are phasing out something old, so people are always wondering who you are and if you are a threat to them.

"I guess my only question is what kind of clients you have here," I said. "I don't like representing cigarette companies or pharmaceutical groups. I mean, I don't mind, but I don't like it."

"Well, we're not in the habit of turning people away," he said. "After all, we like getting paid. Don't you?"

"I don't like getting paid," I said. "I just need it."

That was it for me. He reached into his desk, pulled out a business card, and handed it to me. "If you have any other questions, please email. Otherwise, we've got some other people to see. We'll be making a decision next week. I'll walk you to the elevator."

We walked quickly to the elevator with all eyes in the office on me, though not directly. He smiled, shook my hand, and left before the doors opened.

Back on the street, jobless among thousands of people running around either looking for work or looking to get back to work, I felt even more alone. There was nothing waiting for me uptown other than those damn buildings I had worked so hard to protect.

On the way home, there were no characters with stories for me, only my own thoughts. I got off the train in my best clothes, which put me out of place on my block for that time of day. I saw Armando dash across the street to go work on one of his other buildings. Just as I was about to enter my building, I heard a familiar voice, but it did not match the body I was missing. It was the girl from across the block.

"You need any company?" she inquired. "Figured you might be getting lonely up there and needing a home-cooked meal right about now."

"The only person I ever needed is gone," I said. "Leave me alone."

"Alone's no way to be," she replied.

"It's the only thing I want," I told her, moving into the vestibule. She hung her head and slunk away like a wounded animal. I looked up on the steps and saw a woman wearing a green bomber jacket with the furry hood flipped over her head.

"You just couldn't live without me, I guess?" said the voice. She flipped back the hood and nearly gave me a heart attack.

It was Namuna.

"How? How??!" I cried.

She smiled and said nothing. I ran to her and grabbed her quick, not wanting to lose the moment by having her explain.

"I can tell you everything. Come on, let's go upstairs."

7

"I had to make you see what you needed," she said.

"Where were you, then?" I asked. "Don't you know what you put me through?"

"I guess something like you put me through with that woman across the street," she said, looking around at how filthy the apartment was. "I was away on a gig, one that paid enough for us just to be together, no work, no distractions. Can't we just do that for now? What happened in here?"

"I've been working at the garden with Crossing Guard Lita and bringing some of it home with me," I said.

"Why don't you put those shovels away, and I'll clean up this dirt. You really went to pieces without me."

"You're my life," I said.

"And now you realize that."

Knight walked in and brushed himself up against the leg of the chair Namuna was sitting on.

"The Reporter said you were . . . he has footage."

"Did you ever watch it?" she asked. "No, I guess you wouldn't. But it doesn't matter. We're going to be together now, no matter what. That's enough, isn't it?"

"It is," I said. "Though you almost killed me, putting me through it all."

"But you made it, right? And now we can be together without the burden of our past weighing down the future."

There was a shout from the block below. I opened the window and saw the Bodega Guy yelling at me from across the street.

"I got beers waiting, my man," he yelled. "Come on down."

"Not tonight," I yelled back. "I'm making up for lost time."

I closed the window and drew the curtains. I put on WBGO and let whatever the DJ had in his heart provide the soundtrack for our reunion. We danced together in the middle of the living room, like we did when we first got to Harlem, with no furniture and only the hope of each other.

I didn't sleep that evening after we made love. I just watched her until the sun came up and slept next to her the rest of the day after that. I was relaxed for the first time since what I thought was her accident.

We did this over and over again. I became a little bit protective of her, bordering on controlling, but she liked it. I thought she did, anyway. I never wanted her to leave the house, so when we needed food, we'd either order in or I'd go down the block to the Foodtown to pick up groceries. On my walks up and down the block, I now noticed the change in the neighborhood. The streets were clean and the carts that lined up on the block were full of fruits, juice with coconut milk, original pieces of art, kids selling their CDs, asking you to just take a minute and put on the headphones, and, of course, chicken and rice. I guess I had made a difference, but the cause of the pride and pleasure I carried with me was back in the apartment.

As I was bringing up some bread and pasta for dinner one night, the young guy in the next apartment was opening his door. He looked like he wanted to say something to me but only gave me a strange look, almost like pity, then walked in to his wife. I guess I understand why he might feel that way toward me. I mean, there I was, gray-haired, moving a little slow up the stairs, and carrying a bag of basic groceries into my apartment. I was no great man to him, but everything for me was on the other side of the door.

Funny that a young couple now lived next door, and to them I was a man who seemed to have lost everything, rattling around inside an old Harlem apartment.

8

I was fast asleep on a Sunday morning when the heavy knocking woke me up. Namuna stayed asleep and I went to the door. Through the peephole I saw Armando standing there with my neighbors and the Reporter.

"Open it the door," Armando yelled. "You need to open!"

"What are you doing here so early?" I asked all of them. "Something wrong?"

"That's what we're here to ask you," said the Reporter, making his way past me and into the hallway before stopping midway to hold his nose and turn back.

"What the hell happened to you?" he said.

"Quiet. You'll wake her," I said, closing the bedroom door to keep Namuna from waking up. "What's the problem?"

They all looked shocked.

"How long has she been here?" Armando asked.

"About a month," I said. "What business is it of yours?"

"What do you mean?" the neighbor said. "Can't you smell that? How can you live with the smell? I can't. I thought maybe it was a rat in the wall or something, but it just kept getting stronger and stronger. I had no idea what it was."

He turned his head out to the hall and started gagging. I could see his back heaving in the doorway.

"You need her out. Now," Armando said. "I know it's been hard on you losing her like that, but she can't stay it here. It's not human. I'm calling the police if you don't take care of it right now!"

He slammed the door behind him as he exited.

"What the hell is wrong with them?" I asked the Reporter.

"You can't see it?" the Reporter asked, covering his mouth and nose with a handkerchief. "What about all the flies and bugs? Look at the roaches walking around!"

"The seasons are changing," I said. "That's nothing new around here. When did you get so squeamish? Come on, let's have some coffee before she wakes up."

We walked through the hallway and into the kitchen. The place was dirtier than I remembered. The dishes were stacked high, and the garbage was falling out of the bin.

"I guess I've been neglecting the housework since she got back," I said, laughing.

He didn't say a word. In the silence, in his presence, I started to notice more and more trash around the house. I saw mice running around. I saw the curtains closed and heard the radio playing static instead of the beautiful music that had lulled Namuna and me to sleep since she came back.

The reality of the situation began to come into focus. Now I smelled it. There was dirt all over the floor and a shovel leaning up against the kitchen wall. I saw the Reporter noticing it as well and putting it together as I did.

"What did I do?" I said, starting to rush into the bedroom before he stopped me and held me back with everything he had inside of him.

"You lost a love and tried to bring her back."

"But she came back, didn't she?" I asked.

"Only her body," he said.

Reality came in swift. The smell went up through my nose and into my body, wrapping around my brain like a grappling hook. I walked slowly down the hall and into our bedroom, where I saw what everyone else did:

A body, dug up from the graveyard, that had been decaying and rotting for more than a month.

CHAPTER 17

A LAST DANCE

I couldn't bury her again. Knowing that she was still so close to me, that she was still there for me to touch, I couldn't promise myself that I wouldn't dig her up again.

There was no ceremony for the cremation. I held her ashes inside the urn they gave me over the fire escape and waited for the first decent wind to sweep up St. Nicholas Place.

I followed each speck for as long as I could, until they disappeared. My eyes fell down onto the tour buses that were now moving past with greater regularity. The block was beautiful to everyone but me. The awnings that had been missing for so long were now being put up with the money brought in from the local tax revenues. There was not a one piece of trash on the ground, and each wastebasket was more beautiful than the next.

All around me was everything that I had ever accomplished, but it didn't matter because at the end of each evening, when I closed my eyes, all I saw was what wasn't there. The sounds of ghosts had left, and any belief in a world so empty was impossible to have.

The characters on the block came and went. Some of them never returned. They didn't vanish from my memory, because they were real. They were special only to me—every block, every neighborhood, has those people who hold history in place. There is little history known about the people who take the steps to produce the backdrop for life. I spent the best part of my years thinking I was helping them, thinking that it might lead to some satisfaction in myself.

With these last pages, on the same balcony, I'm finally letting Namuna go. I'm comforted only by the sounds of the Bodega across the street. The sounds of a life that I helped to immortalize, here, on the Last Block in Harlem.

THE END.

ACKNOWLEDGMENTS

Without the following people's contributions and their skill at dealing with my madness in the production of this book, I would be holding nothing more than a stack of papers.

To Jackie Lester, who took the first pass at editing this novel and had the courage to look me in the eye and tell me everything that was wrong and everything that it could be if I just believed in the story, which I did—thanks for dealing with the insane emails, countless questions, and calls filled with doubt. You were the foundation.

To Greg Flores, who always stayed cool in the moment and waited until I sent that last email to finally answer—your vision and design stopped people cold on the street. Hanging off fire escapes makes for the best pics.

To Addison Chan—thanks, Doc. I hope I got the medical stuff right.

To Joy Mazzola, who pretty much ducked and hid inside of her job to make the words bounce as they should—you're aces, coach! Who else would stay on the IM with me through all hours of the night and argue over the stuff that truly matters?

To Giles Farley—thanks for reading it over and over again while trying to get your life in the Ukraine started. Honesty is something that cannot be bought.

To Langston Edwards—not even Hunter S. had a better relationship with his lawyer. Thanks for pulling to the side of the road during a snowstorm to look everything over one more time.

To Tito Nieves—my shaman through the digital world.

To the people of Sugar Hill—especially Jackie Harris for being my window distribution—you gave me my first novel, and I hope I did right by you.

To my mother and father—though you are not together and have not been for some time, it was the combination of the two of you, like it or not, that made me who I am and forced me to get my thoughts out on paper. I love you both.

To Terry Goodman—The Godfather. You took a chance and brought the book from the streets of New York to the world.

To Sarah Tomashek—your soft hands smoothed out the edges that needed to be polished so that everyone could understand the voice.

To Bridget Kinsella and Amy Stewart—the leaders of the miracle-makers squad.

To the people of Melcher Media—your patience and openness in creating the final product made it shine. No more changes, I promise.

To everyone who bought a copy from me when I was walking around the city pitching my heart out—you are as much a part of this book as anyone. Eternal thanks for taking a moment to allow my dream into your lives.

Finally, to my amazing wife, Saruul—without you, my life would not be a life at all. During all of those late nights when I was con-sumed with worry, you calmed me down and let me know that I was on the right path. You are my heart, my life, my soul, my world. Everything is for you.

ABOUT THE AUTHOR

Christopher Herz was born in New York City but grew up bouncing up and down the coast of California.

At the age of eight, after experiencing the reaction of his third-grade class to a story he had written and read aloud, Herz knew he wanted to be a writer. Returning to New York as an adult, he was inspired by his Sugar Hill, Harlem, neighborhood and began drafting his first novel, *The Last Block in Harlem,* as a love letter to his block. Upon finishing the manuscript, Herz left his job and began hand-selling his book throughout the city. Walking the streets each day until he had sold ten copies, he caught the attention of *Publishers Weekly,* which featured Herz in an August 2009 article. Herz also took photos and notes on each buyer's story, and his fascinating collage of readers and contextual vignettes can be seen on his blog, Herz Words.